# HAWKSHEAD

# HAWKSHEAD

JANIS FLORES

DOUBLEDAY & COMPANY, INC.
GARDEN CITY, NEW YORK   1976

All of the characters in this book
are fictitious, and any resemblance
to actual persons, living or dead,
is purely coincidental.

ISBN: 0-385-11364-1
Library of Congress Catalog Card Number 75–17071
Copyright © 1976 by Janis Flores
All Rights Reserved
Printed in the United States of America
*First Edition*

*For Ray,*
*who never doubted*

# HAWKSHEAD

# CHAPTER ONE

"Devon, you simply can't do this!" Cecily wailed to her sister. "A lady's companion! What an odious thought! Mama and Papa would have been appalled!"

"Cecily, you must calm yourself and stop talking in exclamation points," Devon said, more serenely than she felt.

Cecily threw herself into a chair, curls bobbing, amid the clutter of Devon's packing. The room was a jumble of dresses, petticoats, and other scattered apparel. Devon stood among the chaos, one slim finger tapping her cheek as she decided which articles were to be put in her trunk. The girls' maid stood to one side, sobbing quietly and wringing her hands.

"Annie," Devon addressed the latter, "do stop weeping and help me fold these gowns. I must be ready for the carriage at two, and it's nearly noon now."

Cecily sat up in the chair and tried again. "Devon, if you won't listen to me, at least consider poor Edgar's feelings. You know he would love to have you here with us; he's said so, many times." Cecily turned large blue eyes in earnest appeal on her sister.

"Now, Cecily, we've been over this before; I simply refuse to foist myself on your household any longer. Perhaps your spinster sister will come to take care of my nieces and nephews at some future date; for now, I must make my own living."

Cecily blushed becomingly at the mention of future children and said irrelevantly, "If you would only learn to conquer your sharp tongue and unbend a little, you would be surrounded by suitors. Oh, Devon—I don't want you to go!"

"Nonsense. Cecily, if you won't help, I insist you remove yourself so Annie and I can finish packing without distracting pronouncements from you." She smiled to take the sting from her words.

As Cecily flounced out of the room, Devon smiled again, fondly, at her sister's plump back, and her irritation disappeared as she returned to her wardrobe.

Two hours later, the trunk was in the hall, and Devon stood beside it in her brown traveling dress. Cecily had dissolved in tears against Edgar's shoulder, and Devon was hard put not to follow suit. She drew a shuddering breath, thinking she must calm her nerves or she would be in such a state by the time she arrived she would only be able to gibber in front of her new employer.

Cecily turned tearfully to her sister and said, "Oh, Devon, you will write, won't you? And if that woman treats you abominably, please come home."

"Don't be silly, Cecily—of course I'll write. It should be quite an adventure, after all." Devon kept her tone light to forestall any more objections.

"Oh, miss, the carriage is here!" Annie, who had been hovering by one of the front windows, came forward and wrenched open the front door in her excitement. Devon hurriedly embraced Cecily, gave Edgar an affectionate kiss, and swept through the open door.

Her astonishment made her forget for a moment the pain of leaving her only family. The carriage that stood by the door was the most elegant she had ever seen. Gleaming black with shining brass fixtures, it emphasized deep crimson upholstery within. A crest emblazoned the door, a savage hawk's head depicted in the center. The yellow eyes of the hawk seemed to bore into her, and she unconsciously took a step back. A coachman in black and crimson livery scrambled down and opened the carriage door, staring impassively at a point over Devon's shoulder. A groom, in the same livery, stood at the heads of a matched pair of splendid black horses, who stamped and snorted, tossing glossy black manes. Each movement of their finely chiseled heads caused the crimson plumes fastened on the sides of their bridles to wave gracefully.

Even Cecily had stopped her sobbing and was gazing at the carriage in wonder. Devon hurriedly said her good-bys and was assisted into the carriage. The door slammed shut, and with a jolt that threw her back into the soft cushions, the driver cracked his whip and the horses leaped forward, eager to be gone. Pushing her bonnet out of her eyes, Devon had time only for a brief wave before Cecily and Edgar were out of sight.

"Well, I really am on my way, if somewhat spectacularly," Devon thought wryly, trying to calm her fluttering heart.

Now that the flurry of departure was over, Devon had time to think about her future. She knew she had been fortunate in securing employment so quickly; after all, there were many women in "reduced circumstances" forced suddenly to find a means of supporting themselves, and she was just one among them.

When her parents had been killed instantly by the accident of an overturned carriage, her parents' solicitor had been very kind in explaining that there was no inheritance. She could hear the man's dry, crackling voice saying, "My dear Miss Brandwyne, I am afraid your parents were somewhat . . . ah . . . improvident." There had been a substantial amount of money, but it had been used to pay Papa's outstanding debts. Dear Mama, with her liking for jewels and furs and extravagant gowns—not to mention excellent finishing schools for her two daughters—had only to hint to Papa and he showered her with expensive gifts. Devon smiled, thinking of her parents, and how dearly they had loved each other.

Devon was thankful that Cecily had been safely married to Edgar before the accident. Cecily, so loving and generous, but so completely dependent, would have shriveled at the thought of trying to make her own way in the world. Edgar was the perfect husband for her—so dependable and so in love with his young wife. She sighed, thinking that she would have to resign herself to post after post, taking care of old women and perhaps children, since it had become clear that she frightened men away with her forthrightness, and her tendency to lose her temper. Why, oh why could she not learn to be demure and helpless, like Cecily.

Devon had stayed with Edgar and Cecily for almost a year after the death of her parents, but soon felt restless and even worse, useless. She had tried not to intrude on the young couple—and they tried equally hard to include her in everything they did.

In desperation, she finally went to see the solicitor, Mr. Pream, and asked him to help her in securing some sort of position. Mr. Pream seemed to think this was as it should be (Devon wondered what his reaction would have been had Cecily applied for the same assistance) and he set about making inquiries.

Fortunately for her, Mr. Pream lunched at the same club with the solicitors of her new employer. During a casual conversation, Devon was mentioned and immediately an appointment was made to interview her.

Cecily was horrified; Edgar simply shook his head, but Devon kept the appointment, and that day was engaged as a "lady's companion" to Leticia Davencourt, Lord Davencourt's sister-in-law, at Hawkshead, the family home.

And now Devon was on her way there in this elegant carriage. Her thoughts were brought abruptly to the present as the carriage gave a particularly vicious jolt. Fortunately, the coach was well sprung, she thought, as she braced herself in the corner, or else she would have been shaken to pieces long before this. Whatever the reason for this unseemly haste, she added to herself as she readjusted her bonnet and tied the ribbons more firmly under her chin, she hoped that they would all arrive in approximately the same condition as they began.

The harrowing ride continued for several hours and at last, when Devon thought she could suffer no more, she felt the pace slowing imperceptibly. Cautiously, she raised the shade and looked out. Night had come during her sojourn in the carriage, but far ahead she could make out a tiny pinpoint of yellow light. As they raced toward the source of the light, she could make out a figure struggling with huge ironwork gates.

Heavens, she thought as they rapidly approached the still-closed gates, we're going to crash through!

With her head out the window, her bonnet blew to the back of her head; her hair loosened and flew into her eyes and streamed down her back, and she released one hand from the window frame to hold back the strands that were whipping about her face. Briefly she thought how Cecily would cringe before being seen thus, and she laughed aloud at the picture she must make. The wind, cold and sharp-smelling, rushed past her stinging cheeks and brought tears to her eyes.

The gatekeeper flung open the gates just in time for the carriage to flash through, and as they went by, she could see the eyes of the gateman shining whitely in the darkness.

✳☙✳

Finally, she pulled her head back from the window and began a hasty toilette. It would never do to arrive in this condition! But her long dark hair refused to be put back into its smooth coils on the nape of her neck, and groaning in exasperation, she finally bundled it into a thick knot and secured it as best she could with her few remaining pins. She readjusted her bonnet and settled back in the slowing coach, hoping she did not look quite the hoyden she had felt moments before.

At last the carriage came to a halt and she peered out. The coachman jumped down and opened the door. She made her exit a trifle shakily, and was glad of the support of the man's rough hand.

As she looked up at the house, she stared in awe. Hawkshead stood in lonely splendor against the dark night sky. The huge gray slabs of stone from which it was built gave the house a massive solidarity, and it seemed to crouch on the rise of a small knoll like the predatory bird for which it was named. All sharp angles, from the turrets and gables to the tall spires crowning each of the four corners, the house gave the impression of a careful watchfulness. Huge windows flanking the massive front doors had their heavy velvet draperies pulled back, and the yellow light streaming from within gleamed in the darkness like the yellow eyes of a hawk. Devon drew back; there was something sinister about the house, like a huge bird about to unfold its wings and flex its talons in preparation for the hunt.

Don't be ridiculous, she chided herself—you are simply overtired from the journey and imagining things. This is a beautiful, elegant house—there is nothing sinister about it. She stepped bravely forward, trying vainly to smooth the wrinkles from the

front of her dress, and approached the wide semi-circular stone
steps leading to the front door.

Lamps had been lit on either side of the double doors, and by
their light she could see the doors were solid oak, studded with
brass nails. The wood bore heavy carvings, beautifully executed,
and the same crest as that on the carriage was cut into the exact
center. As she stared in fascination at such excellent work-
manship, the doors swung open, cutting the crest equally in two,
and two servants came running out to the carriage.

A tall man in a butler's uniform stood just inside the door. As
she mounted the steps he came forward and announced himself as
Jergens. Devon smiled and received a slight smile in return. Jergens had a kindly face surmounted by thinning white hair, and a
dignified manner. He met her on the steps and offered his arm.

They entered the great hall, where candlelight from several wall
sconces made glowing spots of color on the highly polished wood
floor. The entry was semi-circular, following the pattern of the
steps outside, and had only two chairs, standing against the opposite walls. Directly in front of the entry was a massive curving
staircase, rising to shadows on the second floor. Two short hall-
ways led away in opposite directions from the central entry and
Devon could see doorways leading into the rooms she had
glimpsed from the front. She had the impression of massive ma-
hogany furniture, thick carpets, and shining crystal chandeliers
before her attention was arrested by a silken rustle of skirts coming toward her.

From the hallway to the right a tall, painfully thin woman in
stiff black silk came gliding forward, as though on wheels. Devon
saw a heavy circle of keys dangling from the woman's belted waist
and assumed she must be the housekeeper. This was confirmed as
the woman introduced herself in chilly tones as Mrs. Murphy, the
housekeeper.

Mrs. Murphy was certainly a formidable-looking woman, Devon
thought as she murmured a response to the introduction. The
woman's smooth white hair was severely pulled back into a thin
knot on her neck; icy blue eyes under straight forbidding brows
looked out over a large hooked nose. Her thin-lipped mouth was
arranged in a tight line, while thin bony hands were clasped firmly

in front of her. Her whole appearance suggested extreme displeasure as she stared at Devon.

Devon became painfully conscious of her travel-stained, wrinkled appearance and regretted her impulsiveness in leaning out of the carriage during that last tumultuous advance up the drive. Oh well, it's too late to do anything about that now, she thought, and met that cold blue stare with all the haughtiness she could manage under the circumstances.

She was rescued from the increasingly tense situation by Jergens, who said, "Mrs. Murphy, Miss Brandwyne's trunk has already been sent up to her room . . ."

"Thank you, Jergens," the woman snapped. "Find Lucy and send her to me. Miss Brandwyne, if you please . . ." She gestured toward the stairs, indicating that Devon precede her, and Devon gave a slight nod of thanks before passing her.

The top of the stairway gave way to a hall which was lined with doors. Mrs. Murphy halted before one of them and opened it, leading Devon into a room which had a large fire blazing on the hearth. Several lamps had been lit and the whole effect was welcoming to Devon, who was beginning to feel the strain of travel.

A four-poster bed stood against one wall; several rugs were scattered about the highly polished floor, and a comfortable wing-back chair flanked by a small table with a reading lamp stood in close proximity to the fire. A small desk, a chest of drawers, and a massive carved walnut wardrobe completed the furniture in the room.

Devon turned to Mrs. Murphy and complimented her, saying what a lovely room had been chosen for her.

"Yes it is," returned the woman sourly. "I had suggested another, but Lady Davencourt decided on this one. Her room is directly opposite and I suppose she wanted you near."

Mrs. Murphy's dour manner irritated Devon, but she decided that if she and Mrs. Murphy were to do battle, they would do it some other time than on her first night at Hawkshead. She asked sweetly, "When may I see Lady Davencourt?"

"The Mistress will send for you in the morning. As for tonight, the Master wishes to see you presently in the library; no doubt to instruct you about your new duties." Having delivered this message, the housekeeper turned to go but paused on the threshold and added, "I will send Lucy in fifteen minutes to guide you to the library. I suggest you use the time to refresh yourself—and please be ready when Lucy comes to fetch you. The Master does not like to be kept waiting." With this parting shot, Mrs. Murphy closed the door before an angry Devon could frame a biting reply.

"Well, really!" Devon said to herself, "that woman is impossible!"

Realizing that she was about to meet her new employer, she decided to take the housekeeper's advice and at least wash some of the surface grime from her hands and face. She suddenly felt extremely gritty from her day of travel, and noticing a china washbasin and pitcher arranged on the chest, went over to wash her hands. A mirror hung above the chest and she winced when she happened to glance into it. It was no wonder that the housekeeper had looked at her with such disapproval she thought, as she wiped away a smudge of dirt from the side of her nose.

She sighed, not for the first time wishing that she had Cecily's blond prettiness and round feminine figure. It is certain that I will never be sought after for my beauty, she thought: I am too tall, too slender; my mouth is too wide, my nose too straight. In short, she admitted wryly, nothing seems to fit.

She turned away from the mirror, and taking off her bonnet, began to undo the pins holding the dark untidy knot of hair. It came cascading richly over her shoulders, curling slightly at the ends. Taking up the hairbrush, she brushed her hair and smoothed a wave over each ear before winding the length into a simple coil at the nape of her neck. She opened the trunk which had been left standing in the middle of the room and brought out a simple dark blue woolen dress, smiling as she remembered Cecily's distress at the distinct "governessy" lines of the frock. She had always preferred a slightly tailored look, thinking she looked ridiculous in the flounces and ruffles her sister and many of her friends preferred, and could not make Cecily understand that such clothes were not for her.

Now if I can only assume a little meekness, she thought. I must remember a lady's companion is a paid employee and I have relinquished any former position. She sighed again, this time for the loss of the old way of life, and thought how difficult such an adjustment was going to be for her. Her mother had tried so many times to teach her elder daughter the value of quiet, ladylike behavior, and Devon had really tried to follow her mother's example —only to fall into disgrace time after time for failing to curb her tongue. Poor Mama! It was not from her lack of training that Devon preferred a brisk gallop on a spirited horse to a sedate canter on a hack; nor was the fact that Devon refused to hide her face behind a fan when she could talk intelligently on subjects that were supposed to bore gentle ladies to distraction. Her father had been continually amused by Devon and had said frequently over her mother's lamentations: "Oh, Margaret—the girl has spirit! Would you want her to simper and play coy when she should be herself? God, how I despise pink and white little girls who haven't a thought in their featherheads!"

Margaret Brandwyne would reply, "John, please do not swear. And you forget that Cecily is one of those pink and white fluffs you so despise."

"Nonsense. Cecily has the sense to know her shortcomings— and that makes a difference."

Margaret would roll her eyes and smile at this piece of parental prejudice and John would laugh his great booming laugh.

✳❧✳

Devon was aroused from her introspection by a soft knock on the door. A young girl in apron and mop cap entered and announced herself as Lucy, and if Miss was ready, would she please follow her to the library.

Devon took one last look in the mirror to make certain that she looked presentable; large green eyes stared back at her and she reminded herself that ladies should keep their eyes modestly lowered. Oh, how difficult it was going to be to learn to become subservient!

She smiled at Lucy and said she was ready, trying to calm her sudden nervousness. She simply must make a good impression— how ignominious it would be to fail and have to return to Cecily in disgrace after her first display of real independence!

They descended the stairs and passed through the entry, con-

# CHAPTER TWO

The Master of Hawkshead stood by the blazing fireplace. Devon advanced toward the man, who hadn't moved upon her entrance. She gave a small but graceful curtsy, to which the man inclined his head.

At his request, she seated herself and looked up at the man, who had remained standing. Lord Davencourt was tall and lean, but with a latent strength. He was every inch the aristocrat, from a wide forehead to aquiline nose to full lips, which were now pulled into a small cynical smile. Broad shoulders strained against the fine fabric of his well-cut plum-colored coat; about his throat a snowy cravat was tied carelessly but elegantly, a large pearl pin tucked into its folds. Dark gray breeches encased the firm, well-muscled legs of a horseman, and his black boots were so highly polished she could see tiny flames from the fire reflected in them. His hands were brown and strong with long lean fingers; a ring on his right hand glowed in the firelight, and Devon could see the Hawkshead crest cut into the large golden stone of the ring. He had blue-black hair, one curl of which had fallen onto his forehead, but Devon reflected that it did nothing to soften the harsh lines of his face, nor the hard look in his black eyes as he stared down at her.

"Well, Miss Brandwyne. Do I meet with your approval?" The hint of amusement in his deep voice caused Devon to blush as she realized she had been rudely staring.

"Why, yes . . . I mean . . ." she halted in confusion, and blushed more furiously, hating herself for behaving like a young schoolgirl.

"You are younger than I expected," Lord Davencourt said, his amusement increasing at her discomfiture.

"I am twenty-two, Lord Davencourt," Devon replied, striving to control her voice, which had risen due to her nervousness.

"Hm . . . yes. Well. You will meet my sister-in-law, the Lady Davencourt, tomorrow. I wished this interview with you tonight to explain the circumstances of your employment." He paused and glanced toward the fire, leaving her to ponder this last remark.

"To continue: My sister-in-law has been unwell as of late. Her health is delicate, and when she lost her husband, my brother, last year she suffered a . . . a breakdown. Her physician seems to think she needs more attention, more companionship, to give her an interest again. This will be your responsibility. It is lonely here I suppose, for her, since her health does not permit many visitors. I am often away on business and do not have the time to spend with her that I should like."

This last speech was delivered in a tone that suggested to Devon that Lord Davencourt was impatient with female vaporings and that he did not wish to concern himself with comforting hapless females. She wondered what sort of man he was, to be so cold in attitude toward his brother's wife.

Lord Davencourt seemed to be waiting for some sort of response from her, so she said, "I'll certainly do my best, Lord Davencourt."

"Yes, I expect you will; else I will dispense with your services," Lord Davencourt said curtly. He walked to the door, indicating that the interview was at an end.

Devon managed to find her way to her room again and threw herself into a chair. What an impossibly arrogant man! No wonder Lady Davencourt's health was frail, she thought indignantly; her brother-in-law's lack of sympathy and his boorish attitude probably precipitated a great deal of her ill-health. It was fortunate that he would be away a good deal of the time, or she would be sure to ruin her chances by making some unfortunate remark in defense of Lady Davencourt, she thought grimly.

She was still angry at Lord Davencourt's abrupt manner when she climbed into bed and snuffed the candle. She lay thinking about him for a few minutes, until her eyes were so heavy she could scarcely keep them open. Finally she sank into an exhausted sleep, wondering if she would ever be able to learn subservience; already she felt the first faint prickle of anger at Lord Davencourt's contemptuous attitude, and she had scarcely been in the house for five minutes.

Sometime later, she was roused by a slight rustling noise. She turned restlessly under the covers and opened her eyes sleepily, wondering what it was that had awakened her, but she could see nothing amiss in the dark shadows of her room. Probably just the creakings of an old house settling down in the night, she reassured herself drowsily. She was just dropping off to sleep again when she heard a faint click, as though her door had been opened and then closed softly. But the hours of travel that day had dulled her awareness; it must have been a dream, she thought briefly, as sleep claimed her again. Why would anyone steal into my room to watch me sleeping?

*❊⟡❊*

She woke the next morning to a beautiful day. As she pushed back the draperies, sunlight streamed in. She opened the window and leaned out. She could see the stables off to her right, bustling with activity, and she suddenly yearned for a ride. Sighing, she was about to turn away when she caught sight of the tall figure of Lord Davencourt striding toward the stable. His dark head glistened in the sunlight, and he slapped a riding crop impatiently against his leg as he walked. A fidgeting chestnut mare was brought out by one of the grooms; he mounted lithely and rode off without looking back. Devon had to admire the easy skill with which he handled the prancing horse and watched him until the curve of the drive hid him from her view.

Thank goodness, she thought—at least she wouldn't have to contend with his cynical presence when she met Lady Davencourt.

The summons came as she was finishing the breakfast Lucy had brought to her room. Smoothing her hair with trepidation, she walked across the hall and rapped on the opposite door.

A languid voice bade her enter, and as she opened the door, a wave of heat and eau de cologne assailed her. The room was in darkness except for the light from a small fire and several lamps placed on small tables in the large room. The heavy brocade draperies were firmly closed against the sunlight, and she could barely make out the figure reclining on a couch by the fireplace.

"Lady Davencourt?" she ventured.

"Yes, my dear. Do come closer and be seated," came a faint voice from the couch.

Devon asked if she should open the draperies, but the other woman exclaimed petulantly that the light hurt her eyes. Shrugging, Devon seated herself, already feeling dots of perspiration beading her forehead.

"So, Gareth has decided you are to keep me company," the woman said.

"Gareth?"

"Gareth, Lord Davencourt." Leticia gestured impatiently toward a crystal goblet sitting on the table beside her and Devon hastened to hand it to her.

As the woman sipped from the glass, Devon studied her. Leticia Davencourt was an attractive woman. Her blond hair was arranged in a coronet of braids around her head; blue eyes glowed in a pale creamy complexion unmarred by lines or wrinkles. Only her mouth betrayed a discontented personality, being drawn down at the corners. She was dressed in a white satin morning gown, frothing with lace at the neck and at the edges of the wide sleeves. She stroked a small white cat in her lap with long fingers, and the cat's contented purring could be heard faintly through the room.

Devon exclaimed when she saw the little animal, and the cat turned large, round, green eyes lazily on her.

Lady Davencourt smiled fondly at the creature and said, "This is Kit." At the mention of her name, Kit unfolded herself and stretched languidly, showing small pointed teeth in a yawn.

"What a beautiful cat!" Devon said admiringly.

"You are drawn to cats, Miss Brandwyne? Some people seem to find their independent natures tedious."

"Oh no—I like animals of any kind," Devon replied. "May I pet her?"

"If she will allow it. Kit does not take readily to strangers."

Devon patted her lap, calling to the cat. Kit glanced at her suspiciously for a moment, fluffy tail waving uncertainly. Then abruptly, she jumped from the couch into her lap, circling twice before settling down with a loud purr. Devon stroked the luxuriant fur expertly, and Kit rolled over onto her back, kneading Devon's arm with her soft paws.

"I declare," Lady Davencourt said in a surprised tone. "You certainly have a way with animals! Kit usually ignores everyone who wants to make a fuss over her."

"I think animals know when someone genuinely likes them, don't you think so, Lady Davencourt?"

"I suppose so," Lady Davencourt answered uncertainly. "Well. I will excuse you for now; I'm very tired and I must rest. You can amuse yourself for a few hours, can't you, my dear?"

Devon picked up the cat and returned her to her mistress, then asked if she could do anything for her before she left, but Lady Davencourt waved her away and pulled the bell rope by her side to summon her maid.

Feeling somewhat at a loss with so much time on her hands so soon after her arrival, Devon decided to take a walk. The air in Lady Davencourt's room had been so stifling she felt quite faint— no wonder the woman's health was frail! She would see to it that Lady Davencourt's room was aired frequently, and the draperies opened to admit some light during the day. This wasn't quite as she expected, but at least the woman wasn't an ogre as Cecily had gloomily predicted. Devon quite liked her already, and felt a little sorry for her. Having enjoyed robust good health all her life, she sympathized with those less fortunate. How dreadful it must be to be confined to a few rooms!

She found herself walking toward the stables. She had loved horses all her life, and one of her most wrenching experiences after her mother and father died had been giving up her mare, Chancey. Her father had bought the horse especially for her, and though the mare had been almost uncontrollable due to rough handling by her previous owner, Devon had soon justified her father's confidence in her as a horsewoman. Devon and her father had loved to ride together, and once out of sight of more sedate horsemen, would give the horses their heads and jump and gallop to their hearts' content. Margaret Brandwyne had finally given up admonishing her husband and daughter for their wild rides when she realized her warnings of disaster were falling upon deaf ears.

Devon walked down the length of the stable, stopping at each stall to rub a glossy neck or stroke a velvety muzzle. As she reached the last stall, she could hear restless movement behind the closed door. Glancing around to see if anyone was in sight, she opened the top dividing door, feeling guilty as she did so, for it must be closed for a reason, but she couldn't resist. A lovely bay mare was pacing back and forth inside. When the horse spied Devon, she squealed and rushed to the door, baring her teeth.

"Whoa now . . . easy, easy," Devon murmured softly.

The mare rolled her eyes and jerked her head as Devon reached up to stroke the quivering neck. Devon continued making the soothing sounds that she had learned from her father's old groom —one of the best horse handlers she had ever seen—and gradually the mare quieted. Devon ran her hand over the silken coat, thinking how she would love to ride the creature, when suddenly two grooms came racing toward her shouting, "Miss! Miss! Stay away from that mare! She's vicious!" They were almost incoherent with fear, and the sudden commotion caused the mare to rear in terror. Before Devon could move away, one of the mare's hoofs caught her a glancing blow on the temple. As she fell into unconsciousness, her last sight was of the grooms slamming the top door of the stall, and hearing a terrified whinny from the mare inside.

*❊❖❊*

She woke to hands pressing a cool compress on her forehead. She opened her eyes, forcing herself to ignore a blinding headache, and saw a grim Mrs. Murphy sprinkling eau de cologne on a handkerchief. She tried to sit up but sank back with a groan.

"That will be all, Mrs. Murphy," said Lord Davencourt's voice. Devon winced; it seemed that she would not escape from this escapade with only a lump on the head, she would probably be dismissed as well. And on her first day too!

Mrs. Murphy gathered up the basin and towels and retreated in injured dignity at the abrupt dismissal.

Devon succeeded in reaching a sitting position on her second attempt and gratefully accepted a glass of sherry from Lord Davencourt.

"Well, Miss Brandwyne. It seems you caused quite a stir in my household with your foolishness."

"I am sorry, Lord Davencourt. I . . ."

"What the devil were you about?" Lord Davencourt shouted suddenly, and Devon winced as her headache increased. He continued, "Even the most stupid of my household would know more than to go near a closed horse box with a dangerous animal inside. Do you have any idea of the trouble you have caused?" Anger blazed in his dark eyes and a muscle twitched in the hard jaw as he paused to glare at her. He said furiously, "Now I'll have to have the animal destroyed, since you have assured that no one will go near her!"

"Oh no!" Devon cried without thinking. "Oh no—please! It wasn't her fault. We were getting along famously, before those stupid grooms came running up, shouting. They startled and frightened her, and she reared as a result. It was an accident. Please, you mustn't destroy such a beautiful creature!" She had risen, so great was her agitation, and she clutched the arm of the nearest chair to keep from falling as pain shot through her head, making her dizzy. Lord Davencourt sprang forward to catch her, and she grasped his arm. Dimly, she realized her rashness, but at the moment her only concern was for the unfortunate mare. She looked up into Lord Davencourt's dark eyes and said urgently, "Please—say you won't destroy her!"

An emotion she couldn't identify crossed Lord Davencourt's features: a combination of exasperation, anger, and reluctant admiration, but his expression swiftly changed to one of amusement, and he laughed as he settled her back on the couch. "What a presumptuous minx you are! One of my best mares deals you an injury that frightens everyone but yourself, and then you turn around and insist it wasn't her fault; not only that, but you insist that I should not take measures to correct the situation!"

Devon flushed as she realized how impetuous she had been; she lowered her eyes and waited for the dismissal which would surely follow. Cecily was right; she would never learn to control her tongue.

"All right; I won't destroy the mare. But I hope you realize that I will have to import a new groom to take care of her; all the others are convinced that she is dangerous now."

Devon's relief was so great she felt like bursting into tears. But before she could further disgrace herself, she rose unsteadily and left the room, forgetting entirely that she should wait for Lord Davencourt's permission to leave.

✳❖✳

It was two weeks and more before Devon finally received an opportunity to visit the stables again. During that time, she acquainted herself with Lady Davencourt's daily routine. Leticia rarely rose before ten o'clock in the morning and Devon accustomed herself to supervising the mistress's breakfast tray—over the protests of the maid. She had seen that the trays Lady Davencourt received were sent back almost untouched, and had thought the food was too heavy to tempt a semi-invalid's delicate appetite. Therefore, she had instructed the cook to boil a fresh egg every morning; this accompanied by buttered toast and weak tea were more suited to Leticia's taste. Devon also insisted that the draperies be pulled back every morning, and even opened the window slightly on fair days—much to Mrs. Murphy's horror. The housekeeper insisted the Mistress would take a chill from the draft, but Devon had the couch placed behind a screen to shield Leticia from this possibility.

Lady Davencourt laughed at the housekeeper's protestations and smilingly acceded to Devon's wishes in regard to her own comfort. Faint color began to bloom in the woman's cheeks, and she even felt well enough to descend to the dining hall occasionally after a week of Devon's care. They spent the afternoons reading before Lady Davencourt's rest, so Devon's days were full.

Devon had seen Lord Davencourt but once during this time, as he rose and was away about the estate before dawn. She was in the library, selecting a book for the reading session, when Lord Davencourt came striding in. He seemed to be deep in thought, for when she passed him upon leaving, he barely gave her a nod in response to her greeting.

One day, Leticia announced that she was preparing to have guests for tea. This was an extraordinary event, for Devon had found in the several weeks she had been at Hawkshead that Leticia rarely entertained. Indeed, it had been difficult enough to persuade Leticia to leave her room for short visits downstairs, she thought, as she was summoned to Lady Davencourt's room to assure an anxious Leticia that her gown of lavender silk looked lovely on her. Leticia, pleased by the compliment, insisted that Devon have a free afternoon; she would not be needed, Lady Davencourt said, until the guests had departed.

"That is not necessary, Lady Davencourt. I can easily spend the time sorting through your embroidery basket; you said yourself that Kit had managed to tangle all the threads."

"Nonsense, Devon," Lady Davencourt said kindly. "We can do that some other time. No; I want you to have some time to yourself. You have waited on me constantly since you arrived, and I think at the very least you should take a walk on the terrace. You have been looking very pale these past few days. No, go. I insist."

So Devon went, but the delicious feeling of having the whole afternoon to herself evaporated quickly when she realized she had nothing to do. She threw down the book she was reading in her room and wandered over to the window, wondering how she could possibly fill the suddenly empty hours that stretched before her. Leticia's gesture had been kind; she couldn't realize that Devon was isolated at Hawkshead. She didn't even know anyone hereabout to visit.

The sky outside her window was dark and gray; it looked as though it would rain at any time, so even the possibility of a long walk about the estate to fill the time was denied her. Suddenly, she felt stifled in the house and thought that she could at least take a walk on the terrace as Lady Davencourt had suggested; then if it did rain, she wouldn't be far from shelter. It was better than moping around in her room, she thought wryly, catching up a light cloak and going downstairs.

Once outside, the air was clean and damp; she lifted her face to the sky and breathed in the freshness of it, happy that she had chosen to come outside. She was standing by the low wall surrounding the terrace when she heard carriage wheels on the drive. Not wanting to be caught staring at the arrival of Leticia's guests, she withdrew quickly to the corner of the house just as the carriage drew to a stop at the front door. A coachman in full livery jumped down from his high seat and opened the door smartly.

Devon saw a tall, blond young man leap gracefully from the interior of the carriage and turn to assist someone: a woman, beautifully dressed, but with a hat that shadowed most of her face, stepped out. A slight glimpse of a milk-white profile, a haughty nose, was all Devon could see of the woman before she swept up the front steps, closely followed by the young man.

Devon sighed and leaned against the terrace wall, suddenly depressed. How she missed all those things: beautiful gowns, Papa's handsome carriage and pair of high-stepping grays, calling on friends for tea. Well, she chided herself sternly, those days of leisure are gone forever; it is useless to mourn for things that are all in the past, so she had better accustom herself to looking at such things from the outside.

She knew she should go in; it wouldn't do to be caught lurking about the drawing room windows that opened out onto the terrace. But how ignominious it was to be forced to retire to her room, required to stay out of sight until her mistress called. She wondered again if she would ever learn the meekness required of someone in her position, and thought how difficult it was to pretend to be someone she was not.

She was just about to leave the terrace when a slight grating noise from above caught her attention. Curious, she looked up toward the roof. Her eyes widened in horror. One of the stone globes that decorated the edges of the roof was teetering, moving back and forth as if with a life of its own. She stared at it, transfixed, unable to believe her eyes. Then, with a sudden lurch, the stone tumbled forward, bouncing down the sheltering overhang of the second floor. At the last second, before the stone came crashing down to the terrace, Devon recovered her senses and leaped out of the way. The stone hit the tiles of the terrace with a crash and broke into pieces. Gasping with fright, Devon realized that if she had not heard the stone falling, it would have come down directly on her. Dazed, she looked toward the roof again, as though unwilling to believe how narrowly she had escaped serious injury, and gasped again as she saw a hooded figure staring down at her. It was impossible; the shock was causing her to see things, she told herself. She closed her eyes briefly and when she opened them again, the figure was gone. A trick of my imagination, she thought, relieved. It was absurd to believe that someone had deliberately loosened the stone in order to have it fall on her as she stood below. But she was shaken; it was a few minutes before she could calm herself sufficiently to walk over to the broken pieces of stone.

She was standing looking down at the broken globe, wondering how it came to be loosened from its pedestal, when Mrs. Murphy appeared, gliding calmly toward her.

"What's this?" Mrs. Murphy asked, eying Devon coldly, as though she were personally responsible for the accident.

Devon gestured toward the roof, where it was obvious that one stone globe was missing from the line of its fellows. "Apparently, it came loose somehow and fell," she answered faintly, remembering with a sick feeling the horror she had felt when she had seen it descending on her.

Mrs. Murphy permitted herself a slight gasp of disbelief. "Are you injured?" she asked finally.

Devon shook her head. "Fortunately, I heard the stone as it started to fall, and was able to get out of the way." She shuddered. "What a curious coincidence that it should fall just when I was standing directly under it."

"Yes. Quite," Mrs. Murphy answered coolly, looking up at the roof. "I will inform Lord Davencourt of the accident. I am certain he will want to engage a stonemason to be sure the others are fastened in their place. We had a similar incident not long ago; you have to remember that when a house is almost two centuries old, things like this can happen very easily. But it won't do to have these great globes falling down at whim; someone in the family might be injured."

Devon was about to reply indignantly that she had almost been seriously injured herself, but Mrs. Murphy was already gliding away, presumably to summon someone to remove the mess.

Devon took one last look at the heavy pieces of stone lying broken at her feet and shook her head, trying to forget the narrow escape she had had. It had been a coincidence, hadn't it? And it had been her imagination that conjured the hooded figure looking down at her from the space on the roof where the stone had fallen. Hadn't it?

In her own room again, Devon tried to convince herself a second time that the falling stone had been an accident. She decided she would say nothing about it; she would hate to appear hysterical, imagining things that didn't exist, that someone had deliberately caused the stone to fall. Lady Davencourt would be horrified if she found out about it, and it wouldn't do to upset the delicate health of her employer, especially since her health had improved immeasurably in just a few short weeks. No; for the time being, she would say nothing about it. Say nothing; and try to forget the way in which the stone had grated back and forth on its pedestal as though someone were trying to work it loose.

✳◈✳

One afternoon when Devon came to Lady Davencourt's room, she found Lord Davencourt and Leticia engaged in conversation. She was surprised; this was the first time she had seen Lord Davencourt in Leticia's company. She excused herself and turned to leave, but Leticia said, "Don't go, my dear. I was just saying to Gareth that you hadn't been out of the house for quite a while, and he suggested that you might like to see some of Hawkshead today. Pray do not disappoint me by declining"—Devon had started to refuse—"it would do you good to take some of the fresh air you are always trying to force on me."

Devon glanced at Lord Davencourt, who scowled and turned away. "I am certain that Lord Davencourt has many other matters to attend to, and I would only be in the way," she said, after noting Lord Davencourt's frown.

"Nonsense, my dear. He has to be about the estate himself. Do go and change—I have managed to persuade him a ride would do you both good."

Lord Davencourt did not appear to be agreeable to this persuasion, but Lady Davencourt would listen to no protests, and Devon went reluctantly back to her room to change to her riding habit. Moments later, she was in the stable yard, finding herself anticipating a ride again in spite of Gareth's obvious displeasure.

Lord Davencourt assisted her into the saddle on a fine chestnut mare named Quinzana, while he himself rode a bay stallion called Clarion. They cantered down the drive and Devon abandoned herself to the pleasure of being on a good horse once again. Quinzana was a spirited mare and slyly side-stepped and pranced when Devon slowed her to a walk. She gathered the mare in expertly and laughed to herself as Lord Davencourt had to give Clarion a smart tap with his riding crop to make him behave. The air was crisp, leading to fall, and the animals were restive. Both riders were preoccupied with controlling their mounts and for some time they rode in silence.

Finally, Devon said, "Do you mind a short gallop? This mare is pulling my arms out!"

Lord Davencourt nodded, and Devon touched her heel to Quinzana's flank. The mare gave a leap, impatient to run, which almost unseated her; she quickly balanced herself and gave the mare her head.

As they pounded down the road, she glanced back and laughed again as Clarion reared before following the mare. She heard his hoofbeats coming closer and urged the mare to a faster pace. The wind whistled past her and she leaned closer to the mare's outstretched neck. Quinzana responded with another burst of speed and they flew down the road enjoying the freedom of a good run.

Finally Clarion caught up to her and she reluctantly slowed her horse. Lord Davencourt reached out and grabbed the mare's bridle, forcing them to a halt. Devon looked at him in surprise.

"You could have taken a nasty fall, galloping that fast on a strange horse," he said angrily.

"Why . . ." Devon was so astonished she could only gape at him speechlessly for a moment. Then she said, somewhat piqued at his attitude, "Lord Davencourt, I have been riding since I was a little girl. Quinzana is a spirited horse—you knew that when you ordered her saddled for me. You must have thought I was capable of handling her, else you would have chosen another mount for me."

"She ran away with you."

"On the contrary," she answered indignantly, "she was under control at all times. You indicated yourself that you did not mind a gallop, and Quinzana enjoyed it as much as I did!"

When Lord Davencourt made no immediate reply, Devon glanced at him from under her lashes and thought: whatever is the matter with me? He must think me quite the rudest person he has ever met; after all, he was only concerned for my safety.

Lord Davencourt was obviously controlling himself with great effort. He said tightly, "I would prefer to walk the horses for a time, unless such a pace is too sedate for you?"

"Yes, Lord Davencourt," Devon agreed meekly, unwilling to take the chance of angering him further.

They walked along in silence for a time, when Lord Davencourt said abruptly, "Come this way; there is something you might like to see."

They left the road and started across a field. In the distance she could see a fence, and as they were taking a roundabout way back to the house, she assumed it must be one of the pastures. She recalled that Leticia had mentioned that Gareth was interested in breeding and raising horses, that he had already acquired a reputation among horse fanciers for producing high-quality stock. Indeed, Leticia had exclaimed proudly, the Hawkshead name assured buyers that they were acquiring the product of careful and selective breeding, and people came from miles around for the opportunity of buying one of Gareth's fine horses. Knowing this, Devon assumed it must be one of these horses Lord Davencourt wanted her to see.

As they approached the fence, a neigh greeted them and she could see a black stallion thundering toward them from the opposite end of the pasture. The horse galloped up to the fence and reared dramatically, pawing the air. He was a magnificent animal; coal black, with one white hind fetlock. His perfectly proportioned body rippled with muscular strength as he pawed the ground impatiently.

"Oh—what a beautiful creature!" Devon exclaimed, her eyes shining.

The stallion, as if sensing her admiration, pranced around in a circle, small ears flicking back and forth at the sound of her voice. His shining coat glistened in the sunlight, and when he shook his head proudly, his long ebony mane swished silkily along his arched neck. He came up to the fence and put his head over, flaring his large sensitive nostrils, and snorted a challenge.

Quinzana squealed and turned to kick, obviously displeased at the stallion's audacity, but Devon tightened the reins and moved her mare back again with a well-placed heel. She was too preoccupied with controlling her own horse and admiring the stallion to pay much attention to the quick look of approval Lord Davencourt gave her. She thought she must have mistaken the look, because his face was impassive again, when after soothing her restless mare, she glanced at him with pleasure and said, "I have never seen a finer animal, Lord Davencourt!"

"His name is Onyx," Lord Davencourt replied quietly. "My brother met his death because of him."

"Oh!" Devon's hand flew to her mouth as she gazed first in horror at the man beside her and then at the beautiful creature before her. "Oh, but . . . how horrible!" she finished in confusion, not knowing what to say.

"Yes. It was. Jeffrey—my brother—always envied me possession of Onyx. I forbade him to ride the animal because I knew he was dangerous," Lord Davencourt replied slowly, his eyes on the stallion who was now pacing restlessly back and forth. "I bought him solely for breeding purposes—he has excellent bloodlines. At any rate, I was away for a few days and Jeff, in his cups one night, got it into his head that nothing would do but that he must ride him. The grooms were too afraid to saddle him, so Jeff tried to manage that himself. Unfortunately, he was trying to saddle him in the stall, and Onyx crushed him against the wall. Before anyone could rescue him the horse had trampled him to death."

Devon listened to this tale in mounting horror. Her vivid imagination could picture the scene: Jeffrey, stumbling in his drunkenness, the stallion angered and perhaps afraid, the grooms shouting—all the confusion causing Onyx to seek escape, and finding none, to panic.

She gave a little cry and covered her shaking lips with a gloved hand. Lord Davencourt gave a start, as if forcing his mind back to the present, and observing Devon's white face, said contritely, "Miss Brandwyne, pray forgive me. The details of Jeffrey's death are not for ladies' ears. In fact, the incident almost unhinged Leticia. You see, she was at the stable too, pleading with Jeff to leave Onyx alone. She knew how dangerous the horse could be for she happened to be in the yard when we first brought the horse in. She saw Onyx try to strike down on of the grooms. Sheer temper on his part, but then he is highly strung . . . unfortunately, Jeffrey did not heed her warnings. Leticia has not been the same since."

Gareth was silent for a moment, his dark eyes shadowed as he looked at Onyx. "So that is why I removed the horse to this pasture. I did not want to take the chance of his harming anyone else." He hesitated again before glancing away and adding, "I could not force myself to destroy him."

Devon said nothing, only looked at Gareth with eyes full of sympathy. Gareth saw that look, appeared about to say something, changed his mind, then finally said curtly, "I think we will return to the house now. I have been melancholy enough for one day."

They moved away from the still-pacing stallion. Devon paused to look back at the magnificent animal, and he nickered softly. Poor thing, she thought sadly, he looks so lonely!

After that, whenever she could get away from the house for a time, she would walk to the pasture and visit Onyx. She made no move to touch him, merely stood by the gate observing him. She never tired of watching him prance and preen for her, moving back and forth along the fence which separated them. Gradually, the stallion became used to her, although he would not come near enough to allow her to stroke that glossy neck—preferring her to admire from afar, she thought wryly.

No mention was made of the mare who had accidentally injured her that first day, and she noticed the end stall was empty. Hesitantly, she asked what had happened to the mare, but the grooms had no knowledge of the horse and she was certain that Lord Davencourt had had her destroyed after all.

✳⌘✳

Her days became a comfortable routine. Lady Davencourt seemed to be recovering her health little by little, and Devon was satisfied with her new life. Occasionally she could persuade Leticia to descend to the drawing room for tea in the afternoons. Devon admired this room, with its elegant dark blue velvet draperies, carved furniture, and huge white marble fireplace. A beautiful Aubusson carpet graced the floor in muted pinks and blues, and several rose quartz lamps were placed on occasional tables standing at either end of the brocaded sofa and by the two overstuffed chairs to the side of the fireplace. A large crystal chandelier hung in the center of the high ceiling, but Devon learned that it was lighted on special occasions only.

From the huge drawing room window she could see the elegant grounds to the front of the house. The gardener was kept busy sweeping the fallen leaves of the trees from the carefully tended lawns and trimming the oleander bushes that lined the wide drive from the gates to the front door.

The terrace ran along the sides of the house, where chairs and tables were set in the warm weather. The terrace was without decoration now, as the temperature was too cool for entertaining out of doors. She had once followed the semi-balcony around the house and found that all the rooms on the ground floor opened onto it, until it reached the kitchen area, where she had to take a short flight of steps down to enter the cook's domain.

Devon had long since gotten over the horror of her experience on the terrace when the stone globe had come crashing down on her. The stonemason had been called and after examining the roof declared that many of the globes were loose. He and his assistant had spent several days cementing the rest in place and Devon tried to convince herself that it had been indeed an accident. She was fortunate that she had been aware of it in time to move out of the way, she reassured herself, and tried to ignore the tiny voice inside her that insisted it had been more than coincidence.

Devon had succeeded in persuading Leticia to take an infrequent walk on the terrace, when weather permitted, as it was sheltered from drafts and she thought Lady Davencourt would benefit from the fresh air. But Leticia would take only a few steps before complaining that walking tired her, so Devon did not insist too often. She herself walked there almost daily, admiring the manicured look of the lawns and formal gardens in comparison to the natural look of the small forest and fenced pastures surrounding the grounds.

In contrast to her relatively busy days, the evenings seemed to stretch endlessly and emptily before her. Lady Davencourt rarely felt up to dressing for dinner; it had become her habit to take a dinner tray in her room, and consequently Devon had to accustom herself to a solitary tray in her own room also. After her dinner, she was obliged to read or embroider to keep busy while she counted the minutes before she could reasonably expect to retire for the night. It was difficult for her not to be depressed when she thought of the lively discussions at dinner and then card playing or games afterward that she had enjoyed with her parents and Cecily. She sighed when she realized that her lonely evenings were to become the new pattern of her life.

Then one afternoon, Lady Davencourt announced that Gareth had invited Lady Elinor Chadmoore and her cousin, Courtney, for dinner that evening. She prevailed upon Devon to take her place, as she felt one of her headaches coming on, and wanted Devon to represent her. Devon expressed delight at the unexpected invitation, and while Lady Davencourt was taking her customary rest, spent the afternoon going through her wardrobe deciding what to wear. Were paid companions expected to be drab in contrast to the rest of the company? She rebelled at the thought, but tempered her enthusiasm enough to choose a simple green silk gown. The bodice of the gown was prim enough to satisfy even the strictest conventions toward the conduct of a lady's companion, she thought dryly, as she smoothed the folds of the simply cut dress. She dressed her hair in a different fashion from the smooth coil at the nape of her neck, piling it into curls on her head and threading a matching green ribbon through the waves. Satisfied, she went downstairs and into the drawing room.

When she entered, she noticed that the company had already arrived. Before Gareth could perform the introductions, a young man leaped to his feet and came forward.

"Courtney Chadmoore, at your service, Miss Brandwyne," he said to her, his blue eyes sparkling with pleasure.

"How do you do, Mr. Chadmoore?" Devon replied, a bit self-conscious at the frank appraisal in Courtney's eyes.

Courtney Chadmoore displayed a smooth handsomeness so at home in elegant and wealthy gatherings. From the top of his shining blond head to the polish of his boots, he exuded a sophistication and grace of manner exhibited only by the supremely self-confident. He took Devon's hand in his own and bowed deeply to her.

"Do call me Courtney. It makes things so much less formal, don't you agree?" he said to Devon, looking deep into her eyes.

"Courtney—if I may . . . ?" Lord Davenport interrupted sarcastically.

Devon glanced at Gareth, standing impatiently by the couch. The difference between the two men was marked. Lord Davencourt was as immaculately groomed as always, but whereas Courtney appeared to full advantage in a social gathering, standing out like a colorfully painted butterfly, Gareth Davencourt looked—not ill as ease; no, it was more that he gave the impression of boredom or impatience at the required social amenities—but was too well-bred to show it fully. Devon smiled at Gareth's tight face in amusement, then composed her features at the frown he bestowed on her.

"Courtney!" Gareth said again as Courtney still smiled bemusedly at Devon, apparently loathe to relinquish her hand.

"What? Oh yes, Gareth. Pray forgive me for monopolizing Miss Brandwyne. How remiss of me." Courtney bowed penitently to Gareth, but turned to wink at Devon before taking a step away from her.

"Lady Elinor Chadmoore, may I present Miss Devon Brandwyne," Gareth introduced the two women.

Devon turned to give a curtsy to Lady Chadmoore, who was languidly fanning herself on the couch. Elinor inclined her head graciously, but Devon was startled to see a flash of dislike in the woman's deep blue eyes.

Lady Chadmoore was a beautiful woman; one of the most beautiful Devon had ever seen. Her shining black hair was gathered high on her head in an intricate arrangement of curls and waves with white roses wound through the luxuriant strands; here and there a diamond hair clip sparkled in the light when she moved her head. Her dress was of sapphire blue satin, matching the color of her eyes, with a low neckline that displayed her white shoulders to their best advantage. Diamond and sapphire rings glinted on long slender fingers, which held the white lace fan. After her brief acknowledgment of the introduction, she had snapped the fan shut, but now she opened it and brought it up to her face, fluttering it gracefully and turning that startlingly blue gaze full on Gareth.

Feeling slightly out of place in this elegant company, Devon retreated to a chair placed at the edge of the group and listened to the animated chatter of Lady Elinor with a stiff smile arranged on her features. Lady Elinor completely ignored her, and she winced inwardly when Lord Davencourt responded with a smile when Lady Chadmoore coyly tapped his arm several times during the conversation. She wondered indignantly how it was possible for men to be seduced by such obvious ploys, but by accident, her eyes met Gareth's and she was surprised to read self-mockery in his expression. But no—she must be mistaken, for he smiled again at the simpering Lady Elinor when he looked down at her, and insisted gallantly that she have a little more sherry before they were called to dinner.

Devon was seated next to Courtney at the table and he kept her entertained through the meal by relating highly amusing anecdotes of his adventures abroad. She soon relaxed under Courtney's charming encouragement and even found herself laughing and responding to his stories with a few teasing remarks of her own. She tried not to notice Lady Elinor's condescending silences when Lord Davencourt joined in their laughter, but after a particularly malicious glance toward her from Lady Elinor, she tempered her enthusiasm and sat quietly through the rest of the meal, politely refusing to be drawn into the conversation again.

When the two women left the gentlemen to their after-dinner wine and re-entered the drawing room, Lady Elinor gestured toward the piano and requested Devon to play for her. Devon seated herself and Lady Elinor moved restlessly about the room, a strange expression of discontent upon her beautiful face.

At last she paused by the piano and addressed Devon: "Well, Miss Brandwyne, you certainly seem to have made a conquest this evening; Courtney is positively captivated! But then, he always did have a penchant for servants—why, I remember his narrowly avoiding a delicious scandal with one of the maids in his father's home several years ago!"

Devon was stunned by this malicious remark, but before she could make any reply, Lady Elinor continued, "And Gareth seems to admire your skill as a horsewoman. But of course, I always did consider it poor taste for ladies"—she emphasized the word—"to dash about the countryside trying to compete with men."

Devon was saved from the situation by the entrance of the men. Courtney, upon seeing her sitting at the piano, gallantly entreated her to play for them, but Devon was shaking with rage, all the more furious because she could not respond to the malice still flashing in Lady Elinor's eyes. She knew she could not stay another minute in the same room with Elinor Chadmoore.

Striving to control her quivering voice, she excused herself with the plea of a headache, unable to think of another excuse which would seem more reasonable. She nodded briefly to Lady Elinor, curtsied to Courtney and Gareth, ignoring the quizzical look in the latter's eyes, and left the room with her head held high. As she closed the door, she heard Lady Elinor say, "What on earth has come over you, Gareth, that servants are allowed to sit at table with us?" Elinor laughed merrily, and Devon fled to her room in shame and embarrassment without waiting to hear Gareth's reply.

That should serve to put her in her place thoroughly, she thought as she lay in bed. Her face burned with the memory of Lady Elinor's condescending remarks, as well as her own helplessness in the face of the woman's unfair attack. In the future, she vowed, she would remain safely closeted in her room; Lady Davencourt would just have to make her own excuses or appear herself. She would not be made a fool of again—it was too humiliating!

The next morning Lucy appeared with a note for her. The girl quivered with excitement when she handed the envelope to her. "For you, miss. One of the lads from Foxgrove just this minute brought it over."

"Foxgrove?" Devon asked uncertainly.

"Oh, miss! Foxgrove is the estate of the Chadmoores," Lucy announced importantly. "Do open it!"

Feeling that Lucy's curiosity was excessive, she was about to reprove her, but after glancing at the girl's shining eyes, she decided against it; after all, the girl was young, and there was probably little enough excitement in her life.

The envelope was addressed to "Miss Devon Brandwyne"; the note inside read:

My dear Miss Brandwyne,
Seldom have I enjoyed a more beautiful dinner companion. My only regret is that we did not have more time in which to become acquainted with one another. To remedy the situation, I beg you to allow me to call upon you this afternoon for tea.

COURTNEY CHADMOORE

"Lucy, is the messenger from Foxgrove still here?"

"Oh yes. I thought perhaps there might be a return message," replied the girl, smiling.

"There certainly is."

Devon sat down at the desk, and drawing her writing materials toward her, wrote firmly:

Dear Mr. Chadmoore,
It may have escaped your attention, but I am only an employee at Hawkshead. As such, it is impossible for me to entertain gentlemen callers.

DEVON BRANDWYNE

"Send this message." Devon placed the note in an envelope addressed to Courtney Chadmoore and handed it to Lucy, thinking Courtney's frivolous gesture would be all over the servants' hall by now. How could he do this to her, she fumed; certainly he must be aware of her position at Hawkshead. And if not, he has only to ask his cousin, she thought grimly; she was certain Lady Elinor would not hesitate to give her opinion of her cousin calling to take tea with servants!

# CHAPTER THREE

A few days later her complacent existence was shattered by an incident that both puzzled and frightened her. She had been out walking for a few minutes before going to Lady Davencourt for the customary two hours reading or sewing, and when she returned to her room for a book, she was appalled at the sight.

Every drawer had been pulled out and emptied onto the floor. The few dresses she had brought with her were torn, making them almost irreparable. Her precious books, many of which had been given her by her father, were strewn about the room; even her sewing basket had been emptied, threads and scissors tangled together among the chaos.

Shakily, she sat down in the nearest chair and contemplated the ruin in silence. As her distracted gaze wandered around the room, her eyes fell on the gown she had worn to dinner that one night. The green silk was completely destroyed and she let the material slide through stiff fingers onto the floor while she tried to hold back tears.

Why would anyone do such a thing? *Who* would do such a thing? A touch of fear slipped into her mind and for the first time since her arrival, Hawkshead became more than a little sinister.

She pulled the bell rope to summon Lucy to help her straighten the mess. When the girl appeared, her eyes widened and she gave a shriek that Devon was certain the whole house could hear. She pulled Lucy into the room and shut the door, saying urgently, "Lucy, be quiet! I don't want everyone in an uproar!"

Lucy looked at her with huge eyes, then swallowed and asked, "But, miss! What happened?"

"I don't know, but I intend to find out. Did you see anyone come into my room?"

"Oh no, miss. I've been helping Cook all day until now—I haven't been upstairs since this morning when I brought your tray."

"What about the other servants?"

Lucy turned frightened eyes on her and gasped, "Oh, miss—it would be worth our jobs for any of us to be caught doing something like this! The Master . . . he wouldn't stand for it!"

"I don't mean to accuse anyone, but do you think someone might have seen it happen? I was only gone for a few minutes. There wasn't much time."

"No . . . let me think. I was with Cook; Mrs. Murphy was with us for the past half hour or so. Jane and Mary were polishing the silver; Jergens was standing over them—he's very particular, you know . . ."

"Yes, yes—go on," Devon interrupted impatiently.

Lucy frowned in concentration, then shook her head. "That's all, Miss. Sarah and Martha have their half day off, and Jergens let them go early. I don't think it was any of the lads; they keep out of the house—they get so dirty you know."

It was Devon's turn to frown. Now who—

"Oh, miss! I just thought of . . . no, it wouldn't be."

"What?" Devon asked eagerly.

"Well, a few minutes ago, Lady Chadmoore rode up. Jergens told her the Master wasn't here, but she said she would wait. Just before you called me, he said that he saw her leave—she was in a terrible hurry, he thought, and said she looked upset. But it couldn't be her Ladyship!"

Devon asked quietly, "Why do you say that?"

"Well, because . . . how would she know where your room was? Besides, ladies don't do such things!" Lucy finished in a flurry, proud of her logic.

"I see. Well, it seems as though there's nothing to be done but try and straighten up things as best we can. And, Lucy—I want you to be quiet about this; for the present, I don't want anyone else to know."

She set Lucy to picking up the scattered clothing, while she knelt to gather her books. As she smoothed the crumpled pages, she wondered if Lady Elinor disliked her enough to do this to her. Elinor's actions upon leaving the house were certainly suspicious, but she couldn't believe that Lady Elinor would do such a malicious thing. And for what reason? She decided her dislike of the woman was clouding her judgment, even if her hasty departure from Hawkshead made it seem possible that she might be the guilty party. But for the time being, Devon decided to reserve judgment about Lady Elinor.

It was obvious, she thought, that *someone* was trying to frighten her. Uneasily, she remembered the incident of the stone globe on the terrace. Even admitting that the globe falling almost directly on her could have been a freak accident, the same could not be said for the chaos of the room before her. The rifling of her room was a malicious, childish prank, but what if such pranks became dangerous? She resolved that she would be on her guard against further incidents; but she was determined that whoever was trying to frighten her away would not succeed.

But who was responsible—and why? The questions hammered at her while she and Lucy quietly went about the business of trying to put her room in order again.

It had been too much to expect that Lucy would remain silent; when the girl brought her dinner tray that night, Devon was given the message that the Master wished to see her in the library.

She forced herself to eat calmly and when she had finished made her way downstairs. Lord Davencourt was waiting impatiently in the library. She seated herself at his curt invitation and waited, hands folded in her lap.

"It has come to my notice," he began, drawing his brows into a frown, "that someone was in your room today and that certain of your belongings were destroyed. I have made inquiries, but can find no one who claims to know anything about it. Perhaps you can offer some sort of explanation?"

"No, Lord Davencourt. I cannot. I had been out walking, and when I returned, it was to find my room in . . . disarray."

"Why did you not report it to me immediately?"

"I . . . I do not know. It was so unexpected, I did not know what to do except try to repair the damage."

"Can you think of any reason why someone would want to do such a thing?"

"No!"

"Miss Brandwyne, you are not exerting yourself to be helpful."

"I'm sorry I cannot give you any answers," Devon flared. Her temper was roused by his curt manner of questioning, and she continued recklessly, "It is true I cautioned Lucy to remain quiet about the whole affair until I could try to discover who was responsible, but I can see she did not obey my suggestion. I . . ." Her outburst flailed to a stop at the expression of fury gathering on Lord Davencourt's hard features, and she watched him anxiously.

With a great effort he managed to control himself sufficiently to say tightly, "Miss Brandwyne, it is my concern to find out who is responsible for this malicious act—not yours. All I require from you is to make a list of everything that was destroyed and I will see to it that you are reimbursed." He turned angrily from her and stared into the fire. "That will be all, Miss Brandwyne."

Devon left the room furiously, holding her head high to keep back indignant tears at the abrupt dismissal. After all, she thought angrily, she was the one who had been wronged, he acted as though the whole thing were her fault!

Oh, why does he always make me so *angry*, she asked herself when she was safely in her room. Tears came into her eyes again and she dashed them away with her hand. She snatched up her sewing to occupy her mind with something other than her problems with Gareth Davencourt, but after fumbling with the needle and tangling her thread, she threw it down in disgust and went to the window, staring out blankly with her thoughts in a turmoil. An image of Lord Davencourt swam before her eyes and she saw in her mind the hard, strong line of his jaw, the dark intensity of his eyes. This was a man she could easily fall in love with, she thought dreamily; strong, handsome, capable—and rude, arrogant, cruel, and altogether impossible! she concluded, her temper flaring again. Whatever was coming over her: in love? She was not such a fool, she told herself smugly.

\*⟳\*

Lord Davencourt left the next day for London, or so Lucy informed her when she brought Devon's morning tray. Lucy stayed a moment to chat with her, her whole manner more relaxed now that the Master was away. In fact, the whole household seemed to relax slightly when Lord Davencourt was gone from Hawkshead. When he was in residence, Devon had noticed that the servants moved more quickly, the furniture was polished to an even higher gloss, and the general air was that of expectancy. It was not that Gareth went about shouting at errant servants; it was simply that the Master could demoralize the servants with a word, or one of his black frowns, and everyone preferred not to call attention to themselves by not performing their duties quickly and efficiently. What a soft-spoken tyrant he is, Devon thought disgustedly, as she sipped her tea.

Lady Davencourt seemed agitated when Devon entered her suite of rooms after breakfast. Contrary to her usual manner of reclining on her sitting room couch till afternoon, she was already up, pacing the floor unsteadily. Her rose-colored morning gown swished about her feet as she moved back and forth, twisting her hands.

At Devon's entrance, she turned and exclaimed, her face drawn into lines of anxiety, "Oh, Devon—I'm so sorry! All your things ruined! Oh, who could have done such a thing?"

Devon saw immediately that she must try to calm the woman; Lady Davencourt looked as though she would become hysterical at any moment, and Devon was alarmed. She rushed forward, and taking Leticia's arm, led her gently to a chair. Leticia sat down, holding a trembling hand to her throat.

"You mustn't upset yourself so, Lady Davencourt," Devon said, trying to comfort Leticia. "I'm certain that Lord Davencourt will find out who is responsible."

"Yes, but . . ." Leticia shuddered, and continued, "to have something like that happen in this very house! Why, I shall not be able to sleep at night for fear that someone will come into my room and murder me in my bed!"

"I hardly think that will happen," Devon said soothingly. "But perhaps you would feel better if I slept in here with you." She glanced around the room, and then pointing at the couch, said, "That would serve as a bed . . ."

Devon looked at Leticia and was surprised to see the look of calculation in the woman's eyes; it was gone in an instant, leaving Devon wondering if she had seen it at all. Leticia smiled shakily and patted Devon's hand. "No, no, that will not be necessary, Devon. I . . . I don't feel so frightened now, my dear. You are such a comfort—so steadying!"

Devon smiled at the generous compliment and succeeded in turning the conversation by pointing to Kit, who had been busily tangling herself in a ball of yarn while she and Leticia had been talking. The little cat was such a comical sight that both women laughed, and when Leticia bent down to pick up Kit, her manner once again without tension, Devon hoped that the puzzling incident in her room had been forgotten.

Later that day, when Devon had settled Lady Davencourt for her afternoon rest, Mrs. Murphy appeared in her room. Devon rarely saw the housekeeper, preferring not to subject herself to that icy stare, and since her arrival at Hawkshead, had only chanced to have a few words with that formidable woman. When she concluded that all her overtures of friendship had been rejected by the woman's habitual coldness, Devon had given up the effort to be friendly. She stared at Mrs. Murphy in surprise.

"Lord Davencourt has instructed me to view the damage to your belongings and to repair whatever may need doing," Mrs. Murphy announced grimly.

"That won't be necessary, Mrs. Murphy. I . . ."

"Excuse me, Miss Brandwyne, but those are the Master's orders. If you will give me those gowns"—she indicated the few Devon had been trying halfheartedly to repair—"I will set one of the girls to mending later this afternoon."

The housekeeper stood obdurately, waiting for her to hand over the requested articles. Recognizing defeat, Devon put the dresses in Mrs. Murphy's hands and thanked her for troubling herself. Mrs. Murphy replied curtly: "The Master wished it." She gave a brief nod and departed, leaving an exasperated Devon staring after her.

✳❖✳

Lady Davencourt had taken a slight chill and was confined to her bed; she had fallen asleep while Devon read to her, so Devon was left to her own devices. Feeling stifled in the house, especially since she was no closer to solving the mystery of her overturned room, she decided to take a walk to clear her mind of the troublesome problem.

She put on her warmest cloak—for the past week that Lord Davencourt had been away had been frosty and there was a threat of snow—and hurried out of the house. She closed the great front doors and walked down the drive, giving a sigh of relief at escaping the somber atmosphere of the house.

Suddenly she had the feeling that someone was watching her. She turned to glance back at the house, and as she studied the front windows, she saw an upstairs curtain pulled slightly apart. As the folds of the curtain fell back into place, she was certain that she had seen the white face of the housekeeper, an expression of malice distorting the frozen features.

She shivered and pulled the hood of her cloak closer about her face, sternly admonishing herself not to be frightened. What was there to be frightened of? Mrs. Murphy was likely being nosy, looking to see who would be fool enough to be walking in the cold. Why then, did she feel her uneasiness growing, feel an impending sense of danger? She told herself that she was not the sort who was easily given to fancies, but as she looked back at the house again, it seemed to crouch there on the hill, like a giant bird of prey—waiting. Nonsense, she told herself again—it was just that she had not been out of doors for so long that the gloominess of the house and the change in the weather had affected her.

Soon though, as she walked in the crisp air, she forgot the faint warnings in her mind and gave herself up to the release of exercise. She walked briskly, deliberately taking long strides now that there was no one about who might comment upon how unladylike she was.

She was just about to start back to the house when she heard hoofbeats coming along the road. Soon she could make out the figure of Courtney Chadmoore, cantering easily on a large gray Thoroughbred. She moved to the side of the road, hoping he would ride by, but he reined in his horse as he approached her and made a gallant bow from the saddle. His eyes sparkled as he said, "Miss Brandwyne—what a pleasant surprise!" He dismounted, and throwing the reins over his arm, proceeded to walk with her.

"You know, I was crushed when you refused my invitation for tea. Perhaps I was too precipitous, considering we had barely met; but what better manner of becoming aquainted than over a cup of tea? Surely a most conventional method," he said mischievously.

Devon replied in her most scathing tone, "I can see you do not regret that I became the subject of gossip in the servants' hall through your impulsive gesture, Mr. Chadmoore."

"Oh, come now, Miss Brandwyne. Surely you do not care what stories servants may invent in their idleness?"

"You forget that I hold a somewhat precarious position in that household. I should not care to lose it through some frivolous gesture on your part."

"Are your services so dispensable that you would be dismissed because a gentleman wished to take tea with you? Nonsense! I will speak to Gareth then, if you wish."

"No!"

"Never mind," he said hastily as she turned angrily toward him. "I do not wish to upset you."

"Good. I see we can understand each other after all," she said stiffly, hoping he would take this as a dismissal. She continued walking in the direction of Hawkshead.

"Oh, surely you cannot be longing to return to that forbidding house so soon after meeting so fortuitously?" Courtney said, his spirits unaffected by her stringent manner toward him.

"That was my intention. And I would prefer that you do not describe Hawkshead as a 'forbidding house'—it has many beautiful rooms, and . . ."

Courtney gave a shout of laughter. "Oh, Devon—may I call you Devon?—Gareth surely has not succeeded so soon in garnering a champion for the beauties of his dark mansion? He loves the place —understandable in his position as the heir, I admit—but you! You need light, airy, graceful rooms, and certainly no moribund woman to look after!"

"Really, Mr. Chadmoore!" Devon found herself rushing to the

defense of Hawkshead, its Master, and Lady Davencourt all in the same breath.

Courtney interrupted her tirade by doubling over with mirth. Devon stared at him, astonished, as he leaned against his horse with shaking shoulders. She put her hand on his arm to ask if anything was the matter and in a flash found his arms about her.

"Courtney! Release me at once!" She put her hands on his chest, trying to push him away, but he held her more firmly. As she looked up into his laughing, handsome face, she was startled by the expression in his eyes. Good heavens, she thought—he means to kiss me! Which he promptly did. Mortified by embarrassment—after all, they were standing in the middle of the road—she stood rigid in his embrace.

"I'm sorry, my dear—but I have been longing to do that since I first saw you. Do you know you are even more beautiful when you are angry?"

"Courtney, I am appalled . . . and shocked by your behavior!" Devon sputtered, still struggling to release herself from his arms.

Courtney's eyes sparkled at her discomfiture, which was growing minute by minute. What if someone saw them? What if Lord Davencourt came riding by? She quailed at the thought and said, a trifle desperately, "Courtney, please release me. I simply could not bear it if we were seen."

"All right, my love."

"I am *not* your love!"

"Yes, my dear Miss Brandwyne." Now he was mocking her and she did not know which was worse. But at least he had released her. He gathered the reins, swung into the saddle, and leaned down to whisper wickedly, "Don't worry, my love. I shall come calling properly—no one will learn from my lips of this little adventure in the road."

Before she could frame a stinging reply, he spurred his horse and was away down the road, waving back jauntily.

✳︎✿✳︎

When Devon returned to the house, still unsure whether she should be irritated or amused by the incident with Courtney, Mrs.

Murphy was waiting in the entry. She came forward and handed Devon two large parcels.

"These were delivered to you today; I was just going to have Lucy take them to your room, but perhaps you would care to take charge of them yourself?"

Mrs. Murphy's tone indicated that young women who received mysterious packages were quite byond the pale, and Devon couldn't help smiling at the woman's set expression. Wickedly, she wondered what Mrs. Murphy's reaction would be if she knew about Courtney kissing her in broad daylight on a public road. The housekeeper would probably be completely overcome and brand her as a fallen woman, she thought, as she meekly thanked Mrs. Murphy and hurried upstairs.

Once in the privacy of her room, she threw off her cloak and sat on the bed to open the parcels, forgetting Courtney in her excitement at the unexpected gifts.

The first contained two lengths of fine, soft wool; one dark crimson, the other a beautiful seal brown. Puzzled, she started to open the second box and gasped, as it revealed one of the most beautiful gowns she had ever seen. It was made of heavy satin, apricot in color, with wide bands of the finest hand-worked lace surrounding the billowing skirt. The neckline was so low her face turned pink with embarrassment. She shook out the folds of the skirt and an envelope slid to the floor.

A bold, firm hand had written the note inside. It said:

Dear Miss Brandwyne,

Permit me to offer these in small recompense for that which was destroyed. It was a most regrettable incident and one which I can never repay in full.

My compliments,
Gareth Davencourt

Why did he do this, she stormed, throwing down the dress angrily. He knows I can never accept such a costly gift! The wool would have been sufficient, and certainly not the mocking, flamboyant gesture the gown represented. She grimaced as she pictured the amusement he must have enjoyed in ordering a gown he knew she would have to refuse.

I'll return it to him when he comes back to Hawkshead, she decided firmly; after all, I do have my pride, if nothing else! She folded the gown into its tissue wrappings and put the box into the back of the wardrobe so she wouldn't be reminded of Gareth Davencourt and the low opinion of her he must have to do such a thing.

A little later, she entered Leticia's sitting room and was surprised to hear Mrs. Murphy's voice. She was just about to knock on the half-open door of the bedroom when she heard the housekeeper say: "It's disgraceful! Accepting presents from the Master like any common kitchen maid who doesn't know any better. I think she should be dismissed at once before . . ."

Leticia's calm tones interrupted. "I really don't think it is any of your concern, Mrs. Murphy. After all, what Gareth chooses to do is his own affair."

"But . . ."

"I said that will be all. I will take care of the matter myself," Leticia said with finality.

"Very well." The housekeeper's icy tone indicated her disapproval.

Devon heard the rustle of skirts approaching the door; she knocked quickly as though she had just come in, but the subterfuge was not lost on Mrs. Murphy, who glared malevolently at her as she brushed by. Devon's eyes met those of the housekeeper defiantly, while she forced back the quick words of indignation that came to her lips. How dare that woman spy on me, she thought furiously, staring after the ramrod-straight back of the housekeeper.

"Come in, my dear," Leticia called out.

Devon took a moment to regain her composure before going in; it wouldn't do to let Lady Davencourt see how upset she was that Mrs. Murphy was carrying tales, when she shouldn't have been listening in the first place.

She managed a smile as she walked in. Lady Davencourt regarded her silently for a moment, an expression that Devon couldn't interpret shadowing her face. Finally, Leticia said, "Did you have a nice walk, my dear?"

The question was so totally unexpected that Devon stammered in reply, "What? Oh . . . yes. I met Mr. Chadmoore on the road and we talked for a few minutes," she answered, and immediately wondered what had possessed her to mention her meeting with Courtney Chadmoore.

"Indeed? Courtney can be most charming when he wishes to be, can he not?" Leticia asked, smiling slightly at Devon's confusion.

For an instant, Devon was horrified at the thought of Leticia learning about Courtney kissing her in the middle of the road; but how could she know? she wondered frantically. It was only her guilty conscience that interpreted the innocent remark into something more knowledgeable, she thought, relieved when Leticia did not pursue the matter.

"I'm sure I don't know, Lady Davencourt," she replied stiffly, furious with herself to find that she was blushing.

Lady Davencourt looked at her, smiling enigmatically, and in desperation, Devon asked, "Would you like me to read to you, Lady Davencourt?"

"Yes, that would be nice," Leticia replied. "But first, I would like to say this: I have grown very fond of you, Devon—I would hate to see you make the mistake of attaching too much importance to certain overtures made by men. A young girl can often be swayed by such attentions; to her later dismay, she often discovers that the man in question was only amusing himself." She reached over and patted Devon's hand maternally. "You do understand what I'm trying to say, don't you? I say this only for your own protection."

"Yes, Lady Davencourt," Devon said faintly, too embarrassed to say anything more. She picked up the book and began reading, but her thoughts were far from the page in front of her. Was Lady Davencourt referring to Courtney? Then suddenly she knew: Lady Davencourt was trying to tell her tactfully that Lord Davencourt was the sort of man who would find it highly amusing to play upon her inexperience. Well, she had no intention of allowing herself to fall under his spell, Devon decided firmly; she was not *that* inexperienced! But she was grateful that Lady Davencourt thought enough of her to warn her. How kind she was, Devon thought warmly.

**✳✿✳**

Several days later, the household was in a stir, and Devon surmised Lord Davencourt was home. She met Mrs. Murphy on the stairs and asked her if this was the case. The housekeeper replied that Lord Davencourt was in the library, her expression implying that the whereabouts of the Master were not for his household to question, but Devon ignored her cold stare in her haste. She hurried to the library door and knocked firmly before she lost her courage.

She received permission to enter, and as she did so, Lord Davencourt stood up from behind his desk and murmured a startled, "What the devil . . . ?"

Devon made a brief curtsy and launched into an explanation of why she could not accept the gown he had sent her.

Before he could make any reply, another knock sounded and Jergens entered, carrying a tray with a decanter and one glass. When the butler caught sight of Devon, he turned hastily to Lord Davencourt and said, "Beg pardon, my lord. I did not know you were occupied."

"Quite so, Jergens. It seems my study has suddenly become the meeting place of the household." He glanced sardonically at Devon, who had the grace to blush, and continued, "Bring Miss Brandwyne a little wine."

The butler bowed, left the room, and returned moments later with the requested beverage. As Jergens closed the door behind him again, Lord Davencourt addressed Devon, "Pray sit down, Miss Brandwyne. Let us begin this discussion anew. I confess my mind was occupied with business matters before you accosted me."

Devon flushed again at this none too gentle reminder that she had interrupted him in something important. She supposed she should have thought to ask permission to talk with him, but the deed was done now and she must continue.

"Lord Davencourt, I cannot accept the gown. It is beautiful, but far too expensive for me to keep. It would not be proper."

"Nonsense. Of course you must accept it. It is not a gift you remember; merely an attempt to replace the green gown that was destroyed."

"But I don't recall mentioning that particular gown," she said in confusion.

"Let us say . . . I have my sources of information." He smiled slightly, his face taking on a faintly demonic aspect. "And now that the matter of the gown is settled, will you excuse me?"

He came with her to the door and with his hand on the knob, he stood and looked down at her. "I wanted you to have the gown —not many women can wear that color well, but I think you could do it justice." He opened the door and bowed, but not before Devon saw the intensity in his dark eyes.

Puzzled, she stared at the closed door for several moments. Then she saw a movement from the corner of her eye and turned quickly to find the housekeeper watching her by the stairway. As her startled gaze met the cold eyes of the housekeeper, Mrs. Murphy silently moved away, a strange expression on her features.

Devon felt a faint prickle of alarm. What was the woman about, watching her in this manner? It is quite unnerving, she thought, but if she hopes to frighten me for some reason, she will be disappointed. She laughed to convince herself that her thoughts were absurd, but the sound was more a croak as she hurried up the stairs.

# CHAPTER FOUR

Devon was in the drawing room, fetching a shawl that Lady Davencourt had left there during one of her infrequent visits downstairs, when she heard voices in the hall. Presently, a quick tapping of heels introduced Lady Elinor, who swept into the room before Devon could escape.

Lady Elinor stopped in surprise at seeing her, then in her condescending manner said, "Well, Miss Brandwyne. How is *dear* Leticia? Positively *blooming* under your tender mercies, I vow?"

"Lady Davencourt is well, thank you, Lady Chadmoore. Shall I tell her you are here?" Devon replied through clenched teeth.

"No. No . . . Gareth will be here in a few moments. I sent Jergens to fetch him, knowing he would much prefer my company to his musty old ledgers or whatever it is that keeps him so occupied." Lady Elinor's eyes glittered as she spoke, and Devon had to force herself to remain silent under the woman's patronizing manner.

Lady Elinor laughed brittlely. "But of course, as a servant, you would be unaware of the problems attendant on managing an estate such as this. How remiss of me to address such remarks to you."

Devon abandoned her intention not to be baited, and was about to make an angry retort, but at that moment Gareth came into the room. She held her tongue in his presence, but her eyes flashed dangerously.

Gareth looked from one woman to the other, and as his glance rested on Devon's angry, flushed face, he smiled in some secret amusement before bowing over Elinor's hand and murmuring, "How nice to see you, my dear."

Elinor flashed a triumphant glance at Devon and said languidly, "That will be all, Miss Brandwyne." She smiled brilliantly at Gareth and touched his arm possessively as he stood by her side. Devon noted curiously that though he answered that smile with a curve of his lips, the expression in his eyes remained coldly aloof as he looked down at the woman beside him.

There was nothing for Devon to do but gather up the shawl and leave the room. She heard Elinor remark, "Servants are so impertinent nowadays! Gareth, you really should . . ."

Devon waited to hear no more. In fact, she was so furious she could only think of removing herself from that horrible woman before she created a scene she would regret.

She thought she had succeeded in calming herself by the time she reached Lady Davencourt's room, but apparently her feelings were in evidence when she entered because Lady Davencourt said in surprise, "Devon—whatever is the matter?"

"It's nothing, Lady Davencourt. Here is your shawl." She forced herself to smile pleasantly as she arranged the shawl around Lady Davencourt's shoulders, ignoring Leticia's still-questioning expression.

"Have we a guest downstairs? I thought I heard the door," Leticia said finally, realizing that Devon was not going to tell her the reason she was upset.

"Lady Elinor is here," Devon answered shortly.

"Oh yes. I presume she came to see Gareth?"

"Lady Elinor indicated that she was waiting for Lord Davencourt's return."

They were interrupted by the maid with the tea tray, and after that Lady Davencourt said no more about Lady Elinor. The rest of the afternoon was spent quietly playing cards, while Devon tried to analyze why she should suddenly feel a stab of jealousy at the attention Lord Davencourt paid to Elinor Chadmoore. She was so preoccupied with her thoughts she failed to consider why Leticia looked at her in such a penetrating manner several times during the afternoon.

✳❖✳

Christmas was coming; the household was readying itself for the Christmas ball given yearly at Hawkshead. Everyone was looking forward to the dance since the house had been in mourning the last year, and by necessity, all celebrations had been suspended.

The aroma of fresh baking and the tantalizing odor of spices wafted from the kitchen as the cook, with the assistance of two village girls, plunged into preparations for the feast. The scent of pine vied with the smells from the kitchen as the gardener and his boy cut and brought into the house great armloads of evergreen branches for wreaths and yule logs for the fireplaces. Sprays of holly and even bunches of mistletoe hung in strategic places gave the house a gay holiday atmosphere. There was the noise of running feet, and laughter and giggling from the servant girls as they polished and dusted the great house. Even Mrs. Murphy permitted herself a few wintry smiles as she went about supervising the preparations for the celebration.

Lady Davencourt insisted on coming downstairs to direct the preparation of the ballroom. She seemed to draw on hidden reserves of energy as she tripped lightly about the drawing room, ordering this piece and that piece of furniture removed to the attic, laughing gaily in anticipation, and drawing Devon to one side to recount stories of previous Christmas balls.

"You wouldn't believe it, Devon," she said archly, "but several years ago I was the belle of the ball. I ordered a magnificent gown from Paris, and floated through the evening. I declare, my head was turned with all the compliments I received that night! Why, I remember Gareth was furious that he was only allowed to dance with me but once during the evening!"

Gareth! Devon thought in surprise. Surely she meant Jeffrey. She was confused, poor woman; all this excitement was too much for her. She said quickly, "Lady Davencourt, don't you think it is time for your afternoon rest?" Really, she thought; the bright flush of color on Leticia's pale cheeks was alarming. She must not become overtired and have a relapse.

But Leticia was saying, "Nonsense, my dear! I feel fine. Oh, Gareth!" she called, as she saw Lord Davencourt crossing the hall on his way out. "Gareth, dear, do come and watch the transformation. Isn't this exciting?"

"Lady Davencourt . . ." Devon began.

"My dear, you worry too much. Doesn't she, Gareth?" Leticia asked as Gareth came reluctantly to where they were standing. "But it is so nice to know that you are concerned about me. What you fail to realize is that I am well aware of the limits of my strength."

Leticia turned to Gareth, who stood frowning down at her. "None of your black looks, Gareth. I won't have you spoiling all my fun! I was just telling Devon about that Christmas when you were so upset that you didn't get to dance with me. Do you remember?"

Devon saw the surprise in his eyes; it was there only for a moment, to be replaced by an angry frown. "Leticia . . ."

"Oh, don't try to deny it, Gareth," Leticia said, too quickly. "It was the night my poor Jeffrey drank too much and Jergens and one of the footmen had to carry him upstairs. But it didn't put a damper on our fun, did it, Gareth?"

Lord Davencourt looked helplessly at Devon, who shook her head slightly, indicating that Leticia was becoming overexcited and should be humored. Devon was alarmed at Leticia's brittle manner; she pleaded silently with Gareth for his help. Fortunately, Gareth took the cue.

"Quite right, Leticia; I'd forgotten," he managed to say. "Now, I really think it is time for you to rest. After all, the night of the ball is not far away; you must conserve your strength."

Pleased at what she chose to interpret as his solicitude, Leticia put her hand on his arm and smiled slyly. "Devon, you may stay here and watch; Gareth will help me upstairs. Oh no—I really do insist, my dear. We will manage splendidly."

Devon glanced at Gareth, who shrugged. He offered his arm to Leticia and the two of them left the drawing room, Leticia still chattering too brightly. Devon watched them go, wondering if Leticia's confusion was a symptom of her illness, or if she had simply convinced herself of Gareth's jealousy to prove her own desirability.

Poor woman, she thought. Lord Davencourt's reaction had not been flattering; he had been as surprised at Leticia's pronouncement as Devon herself had been. She resolved that she would treat Lady Davencourt with more consideration in the future as she went to watch the drawing room converted into a ballroom.

The servants pulled back the heavy tapestry covering what she had thought was a wall at one end of the drawing room. When the tapestry had been removed, she saw the two great doors that had been hidden by the drapery. When these doors were opened, a huge room was revealed, magnificent in its elegance. The ceiling was gilded, as were the wall sconces placed at close intervals along the gold and white wallpapered walls. Two crystal chandeliers at each end of the room had been taken down and polished until they sparkled. The parquet floor, of oak edged with walnut, was waxed and buffed to a high gloss. The gold and white draperies that formed an alcove about the raised dais at the end of the room were cleaned and pressed and arranged in elegant folds again about the dais. Gilt chairs were taken from the attic and arranged in groups around small tables along the walls, while a long table was set up in the drawing room in preparation for the refreshments which were to be served. Most of the furniture in the drawing room had been removed, the carpet taken up to make more space for the many guests invited.

The gardener, whose business it was to decorate the ballroom with greenery and flowers, fussed and fumed as two of the servants helped him carry his precious plants into the house from the large greenhouse at the end of the garden. Everyone was warned not to touch the plants he labored so diligently over—he wanted to be certain that they would retain their beauty until after the ball, when he could remove them again to his domain.

Devon received an afternoon off to go into the village and do her Christmas shopping. She bought a gauze scarf for Cecily in her sister's favorite shade of blue, and found some fine linen handkerchiefs she could monogram for Edgar. Her shopping complete, she decided to go along to the inn for a cup of tea before walking back to the house. She strolled along looking in the shop windows, when her attention was arrested by a beautiful green velvet bonnet in the milliner's window. As she stood admiring the flame-colored plume tucked into the crown, a voice behind her said, "Just the bonnet for you, my love—it would match the color of your lovely green eyes perfectly."

She turned and looked into the laughing blue eyes of Courtney. "Courtney Chadmoore—how impertinent!" she said, trying to keep from smiling.

"Now you sound like an old prune-faced governess, Miss Brandwyne," Courtney replied, his eyes glinting wickedly as he tucked her arm through his.

"Mr. Chadmoore, you are making a scene!"

"Nonsense, my dear Devon. However, if I am, it is one of my specialties. Now that I have you in my clutches, you cannot refuse to accompany me to the inn for our long delayed cup of tea," he said teasingly, grasping her arm more firmly.

"I can see you leave me no alternative, Mr. Chadmoore, unless you expect me to arm wrestle you in the street." In spite of herself, she had to smile at his nonsense and added, "Fortunately, I was just on my way to the inn myself."

They spent an hour at a small table by one of the windows at Grey's Inn. Devon found herself enjoying Courtney's company, and the time seemed to fly by. She was surprised at the time her watch revealed when she at last remembered to look at it, and regretfully she told Courtney she must be getting back.

Courtney drove her home and they laughed all the way, Devon thinking she had not enjoyed herself so much in quite a long while. When they reached the house, Courtney became serious and told her he would come again, but Devon, feeling her position as an employee now that the house was before her, demurred firmly.

"I know. You are only a paid companion. You don't have to remind me again and again. At any rate, we shall meet again, my love, no matter how you contrive to avoid me." He stepped down from the trap and held out his arm to assist Devon.

She was gathering her skirts in one hand, preparatory to alighting from the trap when she felt his hands on her waist swinging her down to the ground. He bent and kissed her briefly on the lips before he released her.

She paused to look at him as he swung up into the trap again, admiring his handsome profile and graceful movements, thinking what a fine figure of a man he was. He gathered up the reins and clucked to the horse, smiling and winking at her as he said,

"Don't forget, my love, you will not be easily rid of me. You are far too precious a prize to let slip through my fingers."

She watched him guiding the horse skillfully down the drive until he was out of sight, then turned and hurried up the wide stone steps into the house, wondering why her heart should be pounding so. She had to admit it was pleasant to listen to his extravagant compliments, to be the object of his flattering attention. Could it be that she was falling in love with Courtney? No, she answered herself firmly. The thought was ridiculous. Just because a man handed her a few compliments was no reason to lose her head.

A movement at the darkened drawing room window caught her attention and she was chagrined to see Lord Davencourt turning angrily away from the window. Oh dear, now he is angry with me again, she thought. Then, defiantly: well, I don't care! I can certainly allow Courtney to drive me home on my free afternoon if I so desire. She went into the house, determined to defend her actions, but Lord Davencourt was nowhere in sight. She didn't know whether to be relieved or disappointed as she continued up the stairs to tell Leticia she had returned.

*❊⬦❊*

The ball was to be held Christmas Eve. As that day approached, Devon fell into a depression, thinking that the festivities would be held without her as she hadn't been invited. She thought of Christmases past, when with her parents and Cecily, she had had such gay times. She tried to turn her thoughts away from the memories of decorating the huge Christmas trees her father had insisted upon, of the laughter and whispered conferences and hiding of presents lovingly made or bought, of the house filled with people sharing the festivities of the holiday season. Her loneliness increased and she tried to keep as busy as possible. She and Lady Davencourt spent every afternoon sewing little gifts for the tenants' children on the estate, as this was a family custom, but even this busywork failed to keep her occupied as much as she liked.

The weather had become colder and snow was piled high in drifts, making it difficult for walking, so even this exercise was denied her when her duties with Leticia were finished for the day. Her restlessness increased until even Lady Davencourt noticed.

"Devon, what is the matter?" Leticia asked the day of the ball.

Devon picked up Kit, who was playing lazily with a piece of string she had given her. She turned away from the concern in Leticia's eyes and said, "Why, nothing, madam," hoping Lady Davencourt would not pursue the matter.

"How forgetful of me!" Leticia exclaimed. "I should have given you leave to spend the holiday with your family."

"Oh no, Lady Davencourt; my sister and her husband are spending Christmas with his family. I did not wish to intrude."

"Well, perhaps we can make it up to you tonight."

"Tonight?"

"Yes, of course. At the Christmas ball."

"Why . . . I did not know I was invited."

Leticia looked at her curiously. "But surely Gareth informed you he expected you to be there?"

"No . . ." Devon felt crushed; did Lord Davencourt hold such a low opinion of her that he did not want her to attend the ball? Well, perhaps he was right, she thought sadly—an employee had no business in such a gala occasion.

"Well, whatever the reason for Gareth's bad manners, you are coming. I insist upon it," Leticia said decidedly. "Now, I must rest. Have Lucy bring you hot water and have a relaxing bath— the dancing goes on quite late, and you want to be rested. There will be several young men present. Now run along. I will manage nicely with Mary, so don't worry about me."

Devon said, "Lady Davencourt, I appreciate your wanting to include me, but perhaps Lord Davencourt would not want me to be included since he didn't invite me . . ."

Leticia looked at her archly and said, "Nonsense. I want you to be there, and the matter is settled." She smiled at Devon and waved her away.

Devon turned to leave and heard Lady Davencourt murmur, seemingly to herself, "I can't understand Gareth; I was sure he would include Devon."

Devon's pleasure in being included in the festivities that night was marred by Lady Davencourt's last remark, but when she rang for the hot water and luxuriated in the bath, she decided she would enjoy herself that night, regardless of Gareth Davencourt's attitude.

She was in her robe when Lucy knocked again and came in with a package from Cecily. The note that accompanied it was typical of her sister, she thought, as she read:

Dear Devon,

We haven't heard from you in *ages!* I hope Lady Davencourt is treating you well, and that you are not simply *exhausted* running to fetch fans or smelling salts or whatever it is that rich ladies seem to call for!

If that grim Hawkshead (forbidding name!) is having any kind of festivities, I'm certain you will be there, and although you normally shun this type of thing, I do hope you will wear it. It was dear Mama's, you know, and I know she would want you to have it. And, Devon, if there are any eligible men present, *please* try not to scare them away by uttering any devastating remarks! Remember Mama and her famous raised eyebrow whenever you were about to get yourself into difficulties and you will be all right.

Happy Christmas, Devon dear. Please write and tell me your news. Edgar and I send our love and wish you could be here to celebrate with us.

Love, Cecily

Devon put aside the letter and opened the box. Inside, on a bed of cotton, lay a hair clip glittering with brilliants and small emeralds. So like Cecily to give her something like this, she thought fondly. Well, tonight she would put aside her reservations and follow her sister's advice. After all, she thought defiantly, Christmas comes only once a year, and she could be severe and tailored as much as she wanted after tonight!

She put up her hair in curls and tucked the comb among the waves. When she examined the effect in the mirror, she was surprised to find that the emeralds in the comb caught the sparkle in her eyes, making them a deeper green than usual. Dressing her hair in this fashion made her face appear softer, and two spots of color appeared on her cheeks, giving her skin a rosy glow. She brought out the apricot satin gown Lord Davencourt had given her, and was surprised to find it a perfect fit. The low neckline of the bodice was quite daring for her, but she flung up her head and abandoned her earlier thought of lining it with a lace kerchief. She was twirling in front of the mirror, delighted with the way the skirt billowed out when Lucy appeared.

"Miss, I came to help you dress . . . oh, miss! You look beautiful!" she exclaimed when she saw Devon.

"Thank you, Lucy," Devon replied, pleased at the spark of admiration in Lucy's eyes as the little maid circled around her.

"Oh, the gown is simply elegant—and you've done your hair differently too!"

"Do you like it?" she couldn't help asking.

"Oh yes, miss," Lucy breathed. "You look wonderful! I shouldn't be surprised if you captured all the young men's fancies tonight!"

Devon denied the extravagant praise, but was nevertheless pleased. With Lucy's compliments ringing in her ears, she went downstairs.

❋�><❋

Jergens was standing by the door of the drawing room, waiting for any further guests to arrive so he could formally announce them to Lord Davencourt. He looked as dignified as ever in his crisp black and sparkling white. When Devon paused on the threshold and looked in at the colorful crowd of guests already assembled, he gave her a reassuring smile.

"Do I really look as nervous as that?" she asked, smiling back at him.

"No, Miss Brandwyne. I was thinking that you look especially lovely tonight."

"Thank you, Jergens. I . . ."

At that moment, Courtney caught sight of her and cried, "Devon—here you are at last!" He bounded over to her and took her arm possessively.

Several heads turned in their direction at his outburst and

Devon said under her breath, "Courtney—you are making a display!"

He waved his hand nonchalantly and said gaily, "Oh, don't mind them. They are just jealous that I spotted you first. You are looking uncommonly beautiful tonight, my love, and should resign yourself to the ladies murmuring behind their fans and the men leering, hoping for an introduction. It is only a tribute to your loveliness."

"Courtney, you are being extravagant," she said, trying to act annoyed, but finding herself pleased instead.

"Nonsense," he replied, and tucked her arm in his. They moved into the room where Courtney proceeded to introduce her to so many people she had a difficult time remembering all their names. Courtney seemed to be popular with everyone, although several of the ladies warned Devon that he had the reputation of being somewhat of a rake. Laughingly, she agreed, meanwhile noting that these same ladies went to great trouble to place themselves to best advantage in front of her handsome escort.

Courtney whirled her away to dance and after that she never lacked partners. Finally, out of breath, she begged the stout gentleman who had claimed the next dance that they stop for refreshment. The man tottered happily away and she found a seat in an alcove, sheltered by plants, where she could watch the dance floor without being observed herself.

Her happy smile faded abruptly when she saw Lady Elinor making her entrance during a lull in the dancing. Elinor Chadmoore was more beautiful than ever tonight, Devon thought, watching the woman sweep elegantly into the room. She was wearing a silver gown, the color contrasting sharply with her blue-black hair. Gold threads were woven into the fragile silk and sparkled brilliantly, throwing off rainbows of color as they caught the lights. A diamond necklace glittered on that white throat, and diamonds flashed on her fingers and in her hair. A woman made of ice, Devon thought maliciously, but she was not surprised when Elinor was surrounded instantly by several of the young men, who elbowed each other out of the way for the privilege of bowing over her hand. Lady Elinor greeted these admirers with a brilliant smile and a toss of her head, but Devon saw her eyes wandering over the crowd in search of someone else.

Devon followed the direction of her glance and saw Lord Davencourt making his way through the crowd of guests toward Lady Elinor. This was the first time Devon had seen him all evening and her heart gave a treacherous leap as she looked at him. His dark head shone in the light, and he wore his evening clothes casually and elegantly. His snowy cravat and ruffled white shirt contrasted with his dark eyes and sun-browned face, giving him a slightly satanic look. Easily the most handsome man in the room, in spite of—or perhaps because of—his scorn for the satins and fripperies that many of the men wore, he seemed unaware of the admiring and wistful glances bestowed upon him by most of the unmarried girls present.

He reached Lady Elinor, and her admirers reluctantly moved aside. He bowed over that white hand and Devon saw Elinor give him a playful tap on the arm with her fan. Unaccountably, Devon felt a twinge of envy when Lady Elinor put her hand on Gareth's arm, and they moved forward together to be swallowed in the crowd.

At that moment, Courtney discovered her sitting in the alcove and he laughed as he pulled her to her feet. "Come now—you can't be tired already," he teased. "Although I couldn't blame you —your admirers are increasing as the evening wears on!"

He swung her onto the dance floor, and if he held her a shade too tightly, she pretended not to notice. She concentrated on being charming and gay so that he would remain unaware of the turmoil raging inside her when she caught glimpses of Lord Davencourt bending his dark head close to Lady Elinor as they danced. Not for worlds would she admit, even to herself, that of all the people in that crowded room, the one person she wanted to be admired by was scarcely aware of her existence.

She saw Lady Davencourt sitting on one of the gilt chairs next to a regal-looking woman, and she excused herself from Courtney to join her, thinking it would be a relief to get away from the sight of Gareth and Lady Elinor.

As she came closer to where Leticia was sitting, she noticed that Lady Davencourt was watching someone with narrowed eyes.

Devon followed the direction of her glance and saw that her attention was fixed on Gareth and Lady Elinor, who had paused in their dancing to talk with another couple. Leticia's expression was unguarded in that moment, and Devon was surprised to see that her mouth was drawn into bitter lines, and her blue eyes flashed dangerously as she continued to stare at the handsome couple.

But she must have been mistaken, Devon thought, for as she approached Leticia, the woman looked up at her with a welcoming smile that bore no trace of the bitterness Devon thought she had seen just a moment ago, and patted the chair next to her.

"Well, my dear, are you enjoying the dance?" Lady Davencourt asked when she had seated herself.

"Oh yes. It's wonderful, Lady Davencourt. I hardly recognized the drawing room when I came down—the decorations are so beautiful."

Leticia looked around the crowded room with satisfaction. "Yes, it is nice, isn't it? Oh, Devon, may I present Gareth's aunt, Agatha Moreland?" she said, turning to introduce the woman sitting beside her.

Devon bowed over the hand imperiously extended to her, murmuring a greeting.

That Agatha Moreland had been a beautiful woman in her youth was evident still. Her black hair, shining and thick, was barely streaked with silver; a still firm complexion showed scarcely a line or wrinkle. Her nose, slightly hooked over a full mouth, gave her a patrician air that was wholly compatible with her erect posture and regal tilt of her head. But her most commanding feature, thought Devon, were her eyes. Deep brown, so as to appear almost black, they stared haughtily out from under slightly slanted brows and gazed at the world with an amused disdain.

She was dressed in an old-fashioned purple satin gown, as though uncaring for stylishness. Her lace fichu was pinned by an excellent cameo brooch—the only jewelry she wore—and the tips of her black shoes, just showing beneath the hem of her skirt, were polished, but tiny cracks showed in the fine leather. Strangely enough, this did not detract from the royal air she exuded and Devon thought she would certainly be a forceful personality.

This thought was confirmed when Mrs. Moreland gestured to

Leticia with one finely sculptured hand and said, "Leticia, I would like a word alone with this young woman."

Leticia rose immediately and excused herself, murmuring something about seeing the vicar and his wife coming in. She glanced back uncertainly at Devon for a moment, but Devon smiled reassuringly. Leticia sighed, and with an ineffectual flutter of her hands, went off to greet the new guests.

"Well, Miss Brandwyne, how do you like Hawkshead?" Mrs. Moreland asked, her sharp eyes regarding Devon piercingly.

"It's very beautiful . . ."

"Don't disappoint me, girl—I thought you looked as though you had a brain in that beautiful head. I am not often wrong."

Devon thought that must certainly be true; Agatha Moreland would not permit something so human as a mistake to mar her existence. Aloud, she replied, "What I meant was, it's a very beautiful house, and I consider myself fortunate in finding a position here instead of in some moldy mansion. If one is forced by circumstances to work for a living, don't you agree that pleasant surroundings can make any task less onerous?"

Agatha threw back her head and laughed. "That's more like it, Devon. I knew you would be amusing."

Devon sensed that this woman appreciated a worthy adversary; would think little of someone who would sit meekly by and take abuse, so she said, "I did not intend to be amusing. I was merely pointing out my thoughts on the physical beauties of Hawkshead. If you were seeking a comment upon my employers, I am not in the position to . . ."

"Don't get your back up, my dear." Agatha patted Devon's hand and some of the haughtiness disappeared when she said, "I knew from the minute I saw you—I've been watching you quite some time tonight, you know—that you would be the kind of person to say what you think, not what you might think I would like to hear. How refreshing to find someone who is not afraid of me!"

Devon could sympathize with people who would be afraid of her; her manner and bearing were commanding, and it would be easy to quail before that imperious stare. The arrogance that was found in Gareth Davencourt was mirrored in his aunt, and a family resemblance was strong in both of them.

As if reading her thoughts, Agatha asked, "And what do you think of my nephew?"

Devon colored slightly as she replied, "Why, I think of Lord Davencourt not at all, except as my employer."

"Ah—that is what you would like for me to believe," Agatha said slyly, observing Devon's heightened color.

Unfortunately, at that moment, Gareth appeared in front of them. He bowed over Agatha's hand and said wickedly, "Why, Aunt Agatha, I am surprised you condescended to appear at our little dance. I thought nothing would remove you from your beloved Morehouse but a royal command!"

It was clear there was great affection between these two; Agatha's eyes softened as she looked up at her nephew, but she said briskly, "Gareth, your manners are a disgrace. Would you do me the honor of bidding good evening to Miss Brandwyne and ask her to dance like the gentleman you should be?"

Devon was mortified; Gareth merely looked amused, and Agatha looked pleased with herself. He turned and offered his arm. "Why of course. Miss Brandwyne, may I?"

Devon glared at Agatha, her expression indicating that the woman should mind her own business, but Agatha laughed and waved them away. There was nothing to do but accompany him to the dance floor.

Lord Davencourt bowed to her again and held out his arms. Stiffly, she moved into place. She was certain that there would be murmurs as people caught sight of Leticia's companion dancing with Lord Davencourt, and she flung up her head to hide her unease.

She heard Gareth laugh softly as the music began and she glared at his hard profile, afraid he was mocking her display of defiance. He turned laughing eyes on her and asked, "Miss Brandwyne, are you embarrassed at dancing with me? Your face is quite flushed!"

"Nonsense," she replied sharply, wondering why he always made her feel young and schoolgirlish when she most wanted to appear cool and poised. She turned her head and strove for composure.

They danced in silence for several moments, then Gareth bent his head and murmured, "I knew you would do justice to this gown. I am rarely wrong in such matters."

Devon answered crossly, "How coincidental. Your aunt was just saying the same thing in her own regard."

Gareth laughed softly again, and his arm tightened about her waist. He was an excellent dancer, moving lightly and surely, and finally Devon abandoned herself to the pleasure of being whirled around the dance floor. She closed her eyes briefly and opened them again to look up into the dark eyes now so close to hers. The intensity of his gaze made her catch her breath, and she stumbled slightly in confusion. He caught her so quickly they barely missed a step, and as he briefly held her against him she could feel the hard pounding of his heart. Her own was racing at his nearness, and for a moment she leaned against him, her senses swimming. She felt his strong arms about her and breathed in the clean masculine essense of him and wanted this moment to go on forever.

The dance ended and as the music ceased, she came to her senses and pulled away from him. Her face flamed as she realized how nearly she had made a spectacle of herself. She didn't dare look around for she was certain it had been noticed how close they had been during the last part of the dance. Such a breach of propriety was not to be forgiven, and she could only hope everyone was so concerned with their own affairs, they hadn't time to notice her.

Lord Davencourt stepped away from her and bowed formally. His face had hardened again into impassivity, and the mocking expression in his eyes had returned, leading her to believe that the intensity she had sensed in him moments ago had been wholly her imagination.

She was furious with herself for letting her emotions run away with her common sense; had she really imagined that Gareth Davencourt would have any feeling for her other than common courtesy? The idea was ludicrous, absurd. She, who had always prided herself on her practical, down-to-earth common sense had better dredge some of it up now and stop acting the fool!

Lady Elinor whirled by on the arm of a uniformed man as Devon moved from the floor, and the sight of Elinor was enough to jolt her completely back to reality. Why, she had only to see Gareth and Elinor together to know the man was completely entranced with Elinor's charms. And who could blame him, she conceded reluctantly—Elinor Chadmoore was everything she, Devon, was not: cool, poised, sophisticated; blessed with a beauty that even other women had to admire.

Well, even so, Gareth Davencourt meant nothing to her, she told herself furiously. He was impossibly rude, arrogant, proud, boorish—oh, she could go on and on! When—if—she fell in love with a man he would have none of these qualities. He would be kind, gentle— Oh, what was the use? The kind and gentle men she had met preferred kind and gentle women, which she decidedly was not. And men like Gareth only goaded her quick temper and biting tongue. It was confusing and irritating, and she would put the whole problem from her mind. It was unlikely she would ever have to make such a decision about the type of man she would marry, so she would just refuse to think about it.

Agatha Moreland was beckoning imperiously to her from across the room and there was nothing for Devon to do but make her way to the woman's side. She sat down in a flurry of apricot skirts and tried to control her irritation with herself. She knew her eyes were still flashing and in her mind she could see Mama's raised eyebrow at such lack of control in one of her daughters. The thought made her smile in spite of her annoyance.

Agatha eyed her keenly for several moments, then said, "You look as prickly as a hedgehog. Did my nephew say something outrageous?" She chuckled. "It would be just like him!"

"No, Mrs. Moreland. Lord Davencourt did not say anything untoward. In fact, we spoke hardly at all."

"Ah . . ." Agatha murmured cryptically, and Devon glanced quickly at her, expecting her expression to be mocking. She was startled to see the look of secret satisfaction on the woman's face.

"Have you met Lady Elinor?" Agatha asked after a moment.

Surprised at the sudden change in the conversation, Devon replied shortly, "Yes. I have."

"Your tone indicates that you would have preferred to remain unacquainted."

"Not at all," Devon lied.

"Come, come, my dear," Agatha admonished, and Devon flushed at her own obvious transparency. Agatha continued, "I have known Elinor since she was a small child; she was spoiled then, and she hasn't improved with age." She looked at the object of her remarks who was engaged in vivacious conversation with several gentlemen across the room. Devon followed her glance and her lips tightened. The movement did not escape Agatha's sharp eyes, and she smiled secretly again.

Just then, Lady Elinor broke away from the group and attached herself to Gareth's arm possessively. He interrupted what he had been saying to smile down at her, and Devon turned away from the brilliant smile Elinor gave him in return.

"Poor Gareth. Men can be such fools," Agatha murmured in her ear. "It is obvious Elinor has set her cap for him now that her period of mourning for her husband is over. Although why she didn't marry Gareth in the first place, no one will ever know. They were betrothed once, you know—then Elinor broke the engagement and turned around and married Harry Chadmoore. He was old enough to be her father, they do say—and extremely wealthy. Elinor was always greedy, even as a child."

Devon stared at these revelations. Agatha was nodding cynically and Devon said, knowing she should not be listening to this gossip, but hoping Agatha would continue, "Lady Elinor is a very beautiful woman."

Agatha looked searchingly at her and continued, "Oh yes. If one cares for that sort of brittle beauty. I have never thought it much account however. Some do, I suppose, as she was the toast of London at her coming out. Men were simply falling all over themselves—the fools!—to gain her attention. She led the young men quite a dance before her eyes fell on Gareth. After that, nothing must do but he should join her admirers."

"And did he?" Devon could not stop herself from asking.

"I said they were engaged once, did I not? Oh, Gareth took quite a while to succumb to her charms, but succumb he did. Everyone expected they would marry—it would have been a brilliant match. That is why it was so surprising she should change her mind and marry poor Harry."

"Why do you say poor Harry?"

"Oh, Harry was completely befuddled by Elinor's charms. If she had asked for the moon, Harry would have tried to get it for her. But he simply could not keep the pace, poor dear. Elinor would have them dashing back and forth to London—she feels buried here in the country, so she says—and to Italy and France for the summer season. Parties, galas, the theater, anything for amusement or excitement. Anyway, Harry dropped dead of a heart attack one night at the theater. What a scandal that was! So Elinor came back to Foxgrove—and now she has Gareth in her sights again."

Agatha sighed, then said, "My carriage is coming for me at midnight. I suppose it must be that now." She rose majestically and took Devon's hand. "I want you to come see me, my dear. Morehouse is not as grand as this, but I can promise you it's no moldy mansion."

With this parting shot, she moved away and Devon watched her pause and talk briefly to Gareth. She gave a haughty nod to Lady Elinor, who was still clinging to Gareth's arm, and said something to her which brought an angry flush to that lady's cheek. Agatha laughed and left the room on Gareth's arm, leaving Elinor to stare malevolently after them.

Devon was suddenly overcome by a feeling of exhaustion, and after avoiding Courtney's eyes, made her way to her room, where she sat for a few moments in the darkness. She moved to the window and opened it, breathing in the frosty night air. She was about to turn away when she heard voices below her in the courtyard. Wondering who was there, she leaned slightly out of the window, feeling some embarrassment at her curiosity.

The tall dark figure of Lord Davencourt was below her, pacing tensely back and forth. As she watched, Lady Elinor moved out of the shadows. The moonlight shone on the gold threads in her dress and sent tiny flames dancing in the darkness; the diamonds about her throat glittered in the wintry night, giving Devon another image of a woman made of ice. She came to where Gareth was pacing and put her hand on his arm, saying urgently, "Gareth, I dare not wait much longer. We must be married soon! Oh, darling, I love you—can't you see that?"

Gareth's reply was so low that Devon did not hear, but Lady

Elinor continued, "Why do you hesitate? It will be that much more difficult to explain, although I know I could brazen it out with you at my side! The union of Hawkshead and Foxgrove will give you enough capital to build that silly stud farm you are always talking about—don't you see? You will have everything then—including me!" She threw her arms about him and drew his head down for a lingering kiss. They broke apart at some sound in the courtyard and moved back into the shadows, leaving Devon to contemplate the scene she had just witnessed.

Angrily, she closed the window. It serves you right, she said to herself—eavesdropping can only bring misery to the listener. How many times did Mama tell you that?

She flung herself about the room, jerking pins out of her hair until it was a jumble over her shoulders. She snatched up her hairbrush and brushed until tears of pain came into her eyes. She began plaiting her hair for bed when suddenly her hands were arrested in mid-air. What did Lady Elinor mean when she said, "I dare not wait much longer"?

A suspicion formed in Devon's mind; as it hovered into certainty, she gasped and threw herself onto the bed, not caring that her tears were staining the satin coverlet. Now she knew that Elinor was Gareth's mistress, and that their marriage was inevitable because Elinor would come to him, not only with a wealthy dowry but with his child. Devon sobbed wretchedly, finally admitting to herself that, against all good sense and against her will, she had fallen in love with the Master of Hawkshead. She was all the more miserable because she knew it was impossible; Gareth was bound to Elinor by ties that would forever exclude her.

# CHAPTER FIVE

Christmas Day dawned bright and clear. Lucy chattered gaily as she brought hot water and then the breakfast tray to Devon's room. The mistress expected Devon to accompany her to services, and the carriage would be ready within the hour, Lucy informed her. Life was going on, whether Devon wanted it to or not.

She struggled out of bed and splashed cold water on her face. She glanced in the mirror and hastily looked away from her puffy eyes. Lucy exclaimed, "Oh, I almost forgot. Mr. Chadmoore left a box for you last night." She ran from the room and returned with a beribboned parcel.

Devon frowned. What new indiscretion was this? She pulled the ribbon apart and lifted the lid. The green velvet bonnet she had admired in the milliner's window nestled inside. The short note that accompanied it read:

Devon—don't say you can't accept this. I think it's entirely proper for a gentleman to give a lady something so innocuous as a bonnet. I won't hear of your returning it.

Happy Christmas, my love
Courtney

Devon smiled; Courtney could accurately predict her reaction on occasion—her first instinct had been to send it back. Thoughtfully, she tried it on. The color heightened the green of her eyes, making them a deep jade. Courtney was a dear to remember how she had admired this particular bonnet; she couldn't hurt him by refusing it. She decided she would wear it to church. She was feeling better already.

When she had finished dressing, she went across the hall. Lady Davencourt was waiting with a small package in her hands. She pressed it into Devon's grasp and wished her Merry Christmas. A fine pair of dove-gray gloves was her present from Lady Davencourt and Devon thanked her warmly. Lady Davencourt demurred at her thanks and said she felt so much better since Devon had come that it was little enough to do for her in appreciation.

*❋⟡❋*

The services tired Lady Davencourt and they stayed only a moment afterward. Devon spoke to Courtney briefly while Leticia accepted congratulations on giving such a wonderful ball, and thanked him for the bonnet. His eyes glinted merrily as he complimented her on how becoming the bonnet was, and said he wished he could have given her something more. She did not allow him to continue in that vein, as his ardent expression unnerved her, but climbed hastily into the carriage after Lady Davencourt, waving back at him as they moved away.

When they arrived back at Hawkshead, Leticia went immediately to her room, giving orders to Jergens that she was not to be disturbed by duty calls after the ball, and informed Devon that they would have an informal dinner early in the evening, at which she was expected.

Alone with thoughts that were racing around her mind like squirrels in a cage, Devon decided to take a walk to clear her head. Snatches of the conversation she had overheard between Lady Elinor and Gareth came to her mind unbidden, and she did not want to consider the implications behind them.

She walked toward Onyx's pasture, thinking it had been quite a while since she had been to see the black stallion. Her path lay through a small copse of trees. She had discovered this route accidentally one day and it shortened the distance by several minutes. Snow lay in fluffy drifts under the tall trees, blanketing sound. She walked along, glancing up at the silvery branches, or stopping to examine small animal tracks in the white powder.

She was just beginning to feel more like herself when suddenly she had the feeling she was not alone. Whirling around, she called sharply, "Who's there?" Nothing moved; there was no sound. The trees seemed to close in on her and she could feel her breath starting to come in small gasps.

This is ridiculous, she told herself, there is no reason to be frightened. She must be overtired and imagining things. Resolutely, she continued to walk, nervously noting that the woods were becoming darker. She must have set out from the house later than she had thought.

She was trying to decide whether to return to the house or continue on, when the crackle of a small twig made her jump. It's only a small animal, she reassured herself, forcing her legs to move again. She could scarcely see enough now to follow the path and she decided to return to the house. A sharp snap! of a branch breaking behind her caused her to cry out in her nervousness.

She was certain now; someone *was* following her. And whoever it was, stood between her and the safety of the house! She forced herself to look around and saw a dark shape looming in the increasing twilight. She put a hand over her mouth to stifle the scream rising in her throat; she had already given her position away once—she did not intend to do so again.

Cautiously, she inched toward the dubious shelter of a large bush, dropping to her hands and knees in order to make herself as small a target as possible. Her heart was pounding so she could hardly breathe, and she was sure her assailant could hear its rapid beat.

The dark shape came closer, moving warily among the trees. She could see that he held some kind of club, and her fear increased. She had no means of defense, except her hands, for she knew she was too far from the house for anyone to hear her scream. Slowly, she put her hand to the ground, feeling blindly in the snow for a rock—anything—she could use to defend herself. There was nothing but frozen ground around her and she did not dare move away in case her attacker might see her.

Minutes passed in an agony of waiting while she huddled by the bush. She could hear movement, but did not raise her head to locate her assailant. Finally, she heard branches snapping as whoever had been after her moved clumsily away. She hoped he thought she had somehow escaped from the wood and was retreating. She waited, unmoving, until she could hear branches crackling in the distance. At last, she sensed she was alone.

Stiffly, she tried to stand. Her body felt as though it was frozen from crouching so long in the snow. She rubbed frozen legs to restore circulation and the exertion warmed her enough so that she felt able to walk again.

Keeping as close as possible to the trees, she ran back to the safety of the house, praying that the intruder was truly gone. She crashed through branches and bushes in her headlong flight, stumbling on skirts that had grown heavy with clinging snow.

When the house came into view, she stopped for a moment, gasping for breath. She knew if she went tearing across the snow-covered lawns like a madwoman, a hue and cry would follow and she did not feel up to explanations at the moment. She forced herself to walk calmly, if rapidly, to one of the side doors.

Fortunately, no one was about, as many of the servants had been given a half-day holiday, so she met no one who could inquire about her disheveled and frightened appearance.

Once in the safety of her room, she built up the fire with shaking hands and crept as close as she could to the blaze. Reaction set in, and she had to clench her teeth to stop their chattering.

She pulled off her wet dress and wrapped her warm dressing gown about her, moving a chair close to the fire so she could put her frozen feet on the fender to warm them.

Gradually, she began to feel warm again, a comfort she thought would be denied her forever. The thirty-minute dinner bell startled her and she realized she must have fallen asleep as the heat from the fire warmed her. Reluctantly, she rose to dress for dinner, knowing she would have to find a way to tell Lord Davencourt about her experience in the woods.

She dressed in the new crimson wool, since the dinner was to be informal, and was dismayed to find how pale she looked. Never having had the need for rouge, she did not have any at hand, so she pinched her cheeks to bring out some color. When the mirror returned a pallor unlike her, she knew it was no use and went downstairs shakily.

Lord Davencourt was in the drawing room, which had been restored to order after the festivities of the night before. He offered her a glass of sherry and she was furious to find her hand trembling when she accepted the glass. He cocked an eyebrow but said nothing as a few drops of liquid fell on the table before she could put the glass down.

Fighting for control, she said quietly, "Lord Davencourt, I think you should know that someone followed me tonight as I was walking in the woods."

"Followed you? What do you mean?"

"Well, I was walking there and heard someone behind me. It was becoming dark, so I did not see who it was, but I believe he intended to harm me. He was carrying some kind of club, I think —I'm not certain what it was—"

Lord Davencourt's reaction startled her. He turned fiercely toward her and snapped, "What makes you think that?"

Shaken by his menacing tone, she stammered in reply, "I . . . I could see he was carrying what looked like a large stick or . . ."

"No, no," he interrupted impatiently. "What makes you think someone was following you?"

"Well, when I hid in some bushes, this . . . this person, seemed to be searching for me. He thrashed about for a time, then went away." Even in her ears her explanation sounded ridiculous, but she could not explain her terror or the certainty she had felt that the dark shape had indeed intended to harm her. She looked helplessly at him.

Lord Davencourt's features became even more furious. Thinking his anger was directed at her, she hastened to add, "Perhaps I should not have been walking in those woods. I'm sorry—I did not think to ask permission."

"Don't be ridiculous. You may walk on any part of Hawkshead —without fear, I should have thought!"

"Then . . ."

"You were not injured?" His dark eyes became anxious, then when she shook her head, became angry again. "Why did you not tell me at once? I could have sent my men out to capture this madman—now the game is lost! No one but a fool would remain skulking about, of that I'm certain. Why did you wait to tell me?"

Devon remained silent. Why indeed? She rose from the chair

she had taken and walked to the fire. Staring into the flames, she answered, unaware of the tremble in her voice, "I was walking; I thought someone was following me. I called out, but no one answered. I was so frightened, I could not think. When I finally convinced myself the man—whoever it was—had gone, I ran back to the house. I'm afraid I did not think to tell you at once. It was inexcusable, I can see now, because that will make it difficult for you to find him and punish him for trespassing."

She looked at him with tear-filled eyes, knowing that her clumsiness in handling the incident had angered him. But she was surprised to find him staring at her with a mixture of tenderness and exasperation, before he came to where she was standing. He put his hands on her shoulders.

"Do you think I care about trespassing when you were in danger?" he said quietly. "If I find the man at all, it will be to punish him for frightening you."

His fingers tightened on her shoulders and he added fiercely, "In fact, if he had injured you, I think I would have found him and killed him. Oh, Devon, I . . ."

Leticia's voice interrupted whatever he had been about to say, and Devon wondered at the longing in his voice when he had called her by her name. They moved apart, Devon's face flaming to be caught in this somewhat compromising position. Lord Davencourt glowered as Lady Davencourt said brightly, "I've been standing here some moments, but you two seemed to be . . . preoccupied? Shall we go in to dinner now?"

Leticia kept up a running monologue throughout the meal, commenting on this guest or that at the ball the night before. Devon had never seen her so animated, so talkative, and when she examined Leticia's flushed face for signs of strain or exhaustion, she saw a brittleness about her that was unlike the Leticia who was usually so calm and tranquil. Devon grew faintly alarmed, but thought it best to say nothing.

Leticia's eyes glinted as she made a particularly malicious remark about Lady Elinor, and Devon glanced at Lord Davencourt to determine his reaction. His hard-cut features remained impassive, but though his eyes darkened at the mention of Lady Elinor's name, he made no comment.

Leticia declined dessert and excused herself abruptly, beckoning to Devon. Devon rose to follow, but Lord Davencourt raised his hand and requested that she remain behind. Leticia looked startled, but composed herself quickly and left the room, frowning slightly as she did so.

"I have something for you," Lord Davencourt said as the door closed behind Leticia. "I was going to give it to you earlier, but time did not permit. Happy Christmas, Miss Brandwyne." He laid a small package in front of her.

Devon hesitated, trying to fathom his expression, but his eyes were hooded and she could discern nothing. With shaking fingers, she opened the box and took out a heavy gold brooch. An emerald shimmered in the setting, and she could make out the Hawkshead crest cut into the stone. She raised puzzled eyes to Lord Davencourt, wondering why he chose to give her such a valuable gift.

"I don't understand."

"You have done so much for Leticia, I wanted to show my appreciation in this way . . ."

She didn't know what she wanted him to say, but it was not to speak of appreciation. Appreciation! She said formally, "You are paying me to do what I can for Lady Davencourt; surely that is sufficient?"

"Devil take it!" Gareth shouted in exasperation. "What a proud creature you are!"

"My pride is all I have left, Lord Davencourt. A woman in my circumstances . . ."

"What drivel—and coming from you! I credited you with more intelligence."

"Then perhaps you overestimated your ability to judge," she said boldly, slightly shocked that she could be saying such things.

Gareth's face darkened dangerously. "Nevertheless," he rasped, "I insist you keep the brooch. At least give me the satisfaction of choosing what, and to whom, I give gifts."

"If that is your wish, I will keep it," she replied stiffly.

"Thank you," he said, in a voice heavy with sarcasm.

Feeling dangerously close to tears—it seemed they could never carry on a civil conversation, she thought furiously—she said in a choked voice, "If you will excuse me?"

She walked quickly to the door, but Lord Davencourt was there before her, blocking the way. He seemed to tower over her as they stood there, glaring at each other. Then suddenly, his arms were about her, and she felt his hard mouth on hers.

She had certainly been kissed before, and until now had thought it could be a pleasant sensation or a meaningless manner of expressing affection. How naïve she had been! For the first time, she knew what it was to be kissed by a man—and to respond to that man with a depth of passion she had not known existed. She was shocked to find herself answering his kiss, her arms reaching up to hold him to her.

She could feel the wild pounding of his heart, in a beat that matched her own, and when his mouth moved insistently on hers, she wanted to respond to the passion she felt in him. With a supreme effort, she wrenched away, horrified at her lack of self-control.

"Lord Davencourt!" she managed to gasp. Suddenly her mind was filled with the picture of Gareth and Lady Elinor in the courtyard the night before. She saw the passionate kiss they had exchanged, and her horror at her own conduct changed to fury at his.

"How dare you mock me in this way!" she hissed. "You have no right . . ."

He interrupted swiftly, "Devon, you do not understand. I . . ."

She was so furious with herself and him she did not stay to hear him out. She jerked open the door, ignoring his restraining hand, and fled without a backward glance.

"That . . . that . . . philanderer!" she cried savagely as she paced the floor of her room. She glanced at the brooch she had unknowingly held clutched in her hand in her flight from the dining room. With an expression of distaste, she flung it onto the dresser. Her mouth burned from the touch of his lips and she drew her hand across it as if to wipe away the kiss.

How dare he? How *dare* he! Did he think to trifle with her feelings—that she would find him irresistible? Oh, the colossal conceit of the man! It was not enough that he was involved with Elinor Chadmoore—no, he had to treat her, Devon, like any low-born servant girl who was willing to be fondled by the Master for his pleasure. Well, he would see that she would not be treated in such a casual manner!

She was almost incoherent in her fury, all the more angry because she knew she must accept part of the blame. She cringed when she thought how she had responded to his kiss and this added fuel to her disgust with herself.

She had a good mind to pack her trunk and leave this place at first light, walking if need be. She went to the dresser and jerked open a drawer, pulling out the clothing neatly folded there, but stopped with her hands resting on the lip of the drawer. No. She would not give him the satisfaction of driving her away, like a schoolgirl who had tasted womanhood and was afraid of it. She slammed the drawer shut, biting her lip. Her temper had cooled enough to allow her to try to consider the situation honestly. Was it possible that she had misjudged him? She remembered the wild pounding of his heart beneath her own trembling hand, and the pressure of his lips on hers, hungrily demanding an answering response from her. If he was seeking a momentary pleasure, a meaningless kiss snatched at random, would his embrace have been so passionate, his arms drawing her to him with a fierce longing? But they had both been angry; perhaps in the heat of the moment, he had desired her, had wanted to show his power over her. And he had, she thought with shame, remembering how in spite of herself she had responded to his kiss.

Bleakly, she admitted the truth to herself: Gareth Davencourt was going to marry Elinor Chadmoore; Elinor was going to have his child. Nothing, not even the memory of a precious moment, when they had come together with the same overwhelming longing, would change that. And if Gareth regretted his involvement with Elinor, it was too late.

Sobbing bitterly at this realization, Devon forced herself to admit that it was hopeless. Even more galling was the thought that Lord Davencourt was even now undoubtedly regretting his own lack of control.

No; there was nothing for her to do but make plans to leave. She couldn't bear the thought of meeting him again, of seeing the mockery in his eyes. The memory of that kiss would always be between them, both of them regretting it for different reasons.

But how could she leave? She had an obligation to Lady Davencourt to stay. Besides, she forced herself to admit, she could never tell Leticia the shameful truth that Lord Davencourt had kissed her—and more shameful still, she had responded to that kiss with a passion she had not known existed until she felt his lips on hers.

*❋⟡❋*

The next morning she forced herself to follow her routine. After spending half the night tossing and turning in her crumpled sheets, she had decided that it would be best for her to act as though nothing had happened. Indeed, she told herself savagely, the kiss he had forced on her had probably been forgotten already by Lord Davencourt. It meant nothing to him, and she refused to be forced to give an explanation for her decision to leave while he was looking at her in amused surprise. No—she would just have to wait until an opportunity to leave gracefully presented itself.

She waited impatiently until it was time to go to the kitchen to supervise Leticia's breakfast tray, as was her usual custom.

The house was quite still she noted with surprise when she came out into the hall. Usually, she could hear an occasional murmur of voices as the servants went about their tasks, or a snatch of song from the kitchen as the cook happily went about the business of preparing meals. Today all was silent.

As she entered the kitchen, the cook looked up warily from the table where she was cutting vegetables. "Miss, you do best to be stepping about easy today," the woman addressed her.

"Why, what is the matter?"

"It be said that the Master had a hard night; Jergens was called from his bed to help the Master up the stairs. It's not often the Master is a bit the worse for drink—not like some I've worked for —but there it is; men will have their glasses, and it's not for me to judge." Cook sighed, shaking her head pityingly. "You go back on up; I'll have Mary take the tray this morning. I haven't had time to do the Mistress's breakfast yet, what with the Master wanting one of my special possets, to help his head, like."

With this ominous warning concerning Lord Davencourt's bad-tempered state of mind that morning, Devon hurried up the stairs, hoping to get back to her room before he appeared. As she flew around the corner, she ran right into him. She jumped back as though she had been burned.

"I'm terribly sorry, I wasn't looking," she heard herself say. She looked up at him and her eyes widened.

He was as impeccably groomed as always, but his face had a haggard look that was so unlike him, she was taken aback. Apparently he had cut himself shaving, for a small dab of blood dotted his hard jaw. He eyes burned fiercely above cheekbones that seemed to strain against the skin.

"Are you ill, Lord Davencourt?" she heard herself asking, then could have bitten her tongue as he gave a short laugh.

"In a manner of speaking, yes," he replied mockingly. "You see before you a man slightly the worse for drink. But that is of no account right now. I want to apologize for my ungentlemanly conduct last night. It was quite unforgivable for me to take advantage of . . . a woman in your circumstances." He bowed formally to her and said coldly, "I can assure you, it will not happen again."

He crossed the entry and went out through the front door, shouting for his horse. Moments later she heard the clatter of hoofs against the gravel drive as he rode away.

She stood with clenched fists in the hallway. Well—there! She had his apology, and the promise that a scene such as last night would not happen again. Why then, when she should be elated over her victory, did she feel that something precious had slipped away?

She shook her head, irritated by her conflicting emotions, and went in to bid good morning to Leticia, hoping that her erratic emotions would adjust themselves to their normal decisive course.

Lady Davencourt was still in bed as she entered the stuffy room. Devon could tell it was going to be one of Leticia's bad days, for as soon as Lady Davencourt saw her, she said, "Where have you been? I've been waiting all morning, and no one has had the grace to come near me."

"I'm sorry, Lady Davencourt. Mary will be bringing up the breakfast tray directly, and after you have had something to eat, perhaps I could read you the next chapter . . ."

"I don't want anything to eat, and I'm bored with that book,"

Leticia exclaimed petulantly. "Oh, why do we have to have Christmas? It upsets the whole routine, and takes days for everything to return to normal!"

"But didn't you enjoy the Christmas ball? You looked so lovely in that beautiful gown," Devon said soothingly.

Leticia asked archly, "Do you really think so? Of course, I had to have it ordered specially—I do think it fit perfectly, and was more proper than that distasteful gown Elinor Chadmoore was wearing." Leticia sighed, her good humor restored by Devon's compliments, and the morning passed pleasantly.

❋✧❋

After their encounter in the hall and Gareth's apology, Devon studiously kept out of the way of Lord Davencourt. When they chanced to meet in the house, she gave a brief curtsy, he a curt nod, and they passed without speaking. Yet, in spite of herself, Devon found herself listening for his return, and would hide shamelessly behind the curtains in her room, peeping down into the stable yard to catch a glimpse of his dark head whenever he returned to the house.

This is intolerable, she fumed. She must leave; return to her sister, pride in rags if need be, but she must get away from the sight of him. She berated herself for behaving like a schoolgirl with an infatuation. You are a fool, she chided herself endlessly. Why should he look at you when Lady Elinor, who has so much more to offer, is practically throwing herself at him? Their marriage was inevitable she knew. Well, she would not remain for *that* event, she told herself decidedly. She would leave as soon as possible.

But she was still in her state of indecision when one week after the Christmas ball, she received an invitation from Agatha Moreland to take tea with her. The invitation was couched in such commanding terms that Devon reflected wryly it was more an order to appear than a polite request for her company. But to her surprise, she found she was looking forward to a visit with Gareth's imposing aunt, and she set off on her next free afternoon for Morehouse, being certain to send advance warning of her visit.

As she approached the house, she saw that it was not nearly as large as Hawkshead, nor did it give the impression of a forbidding brooding mansion. Instead, she had to admire the small manor house, which stood in isolation amid informal but well-kept grounds. It was a comfortable-looking place, made more so by the faded red brick of which it was built, and the sloping roof which gave it the appearance of a hen squatting comfortably in her nest.

She approached the weathered oak door and raised the brass knocker with slight trepidation. A brisk maid answered the door and before long Devon was ushered into a cozy parlor where Mrs. Moreland sat busy with her needlework.

Agatha looked up at her entrance and said, "I'm pleased you decided to accept my invitation, Miss Brandwyne. Come, be seated."

The tea was brought in and Agatha poured for her guest, then sat back and regarded her piercingly. "I believe you have lost some of your color since I last saw you, Devon. Are you pining away in our country atmosphere—or is Leticia more burdensome than usual?"

Devon was surprised that Mrs. Moreland should speak so of Lady Davencourt. Her expression must have indicated her astonishment, for Agatha laughed and continued crisply, "You wonder that I do not sympathize with poor Leticia's ill-health? I confess I do find her constant vaporings irksome—especially since most of it is in her head!"

"Oh no, Mrs. Moreland," Devon defended, "Lady Davencourt's health is indeed frail—"

"The only thing that's frail about Leticia Davencourt is her brain," Agatha replied cuttingly. "However, I did not ask you to tea to discuss Leticia. I find that as a subject for conversation, she is exceedingly boring."

Thinking that Agatha had certainly given her opinion regarding Leticia in less than civil terms, Devon had to smile at the autocratic manner of the woman sitting opposite her.

Agatha said, with satisfaction, "I can see you have a tendency to agree with me—whether you want to admit it or not."

"No, I cannot quite agree with you, Mrs. Moreland," Devon replied daringly. "Lady Davencourt has been very kind to me. It is not her fault that her constitution is not as strong as those of us more fortunate in health . . ."

Agatha gave a bark of laughter. "I knew you would bring a breath of fresh air to all of us! What a time your poor mama must have had with you. Do you always speak your mind, regardless of the social consequences? Yes, I can see that you do," she said, before Devon could defend herself. "How refreshing! I'll wager that you've set more than one person on his ears at Hawkshead during your stay!"

Devon decidedly did not care for the turn in conversation, feeling herself at a distinct disadvantage in the face of Agatha's shrewd appraisal.

She looked away from Agatha in confusion and her glance fell on a portrait hanging above the mantel. She had been too preoccupied to give notice to it earlier, and as she gazed at it now she wondered that she had failed to see it before.

The portrait was of a young woman in a green riding habit. She stood with her dark head flung up, one gloved hand holding the reins of a beautiful bay mare with easy grace. The figure was tall and slender, erect with the natural proud bearing of self-confidence and good breeding. The eyes of the young woman were her most arresting feature; they glowed with intelligence and self-possession, indicating that their owner would be in complete command of any situation.

Devon glanced at Agatha, who was looking at the portrait with a pensive expression. "Who is the young woman in the portrait?" Devon asked softly.

"My daughter, Damaris," Agatha replied, looking away from the painting and calmly pouring herself another cup. "She was twenty when she died eight years ago—the same age as Gareth. In fact, they were together when it happened. Poor Gareth—it took quite a long while for him to get over the shock of her death . . ."

"I'm terribly sorry, Mrs. Moreland," Devon said sympathetically. "It must have been quite a shock for you too—such a beautiful young woman."

"Yes," Agatha said briefly, looking up at the picture again. "The horse in the painting was her favorite. They were a pair, I can tell you—both stubborn, both spirited. At any rate, Gareth and Damaris were out riding one day—taking jumps at their usual breakneck speed. Damaris' horse fell . . . she was killed instantly."

Tears shone briefly in Agatha's eyes before she could exert her normal, calm self-control. Pressing her lips together as though to repudiate such weakness, she continued briskly, "Gareth, of course, felt he was to blame—which was ridiculous; Damaris was a headstrong young woman. Nothing he could have said to deter her would have made any difference. In many ways, you remind me of her, Devon." Agatha looked at Devon so intently that she was certain Agatha had told her the sad tale of her daughter's death for the purpose of warning her about her own headstrong ways. It was a lesson well taken, she thought, looking up at the portrait of Damaris Moreland.

"Well," Agatha said briskly. "On your next visit we will talk of happier things. I expect to see much of you, my dear—this old house needs a young face now and again to brighten us up. I hope I will not have to ask formally for your company next time."

Agatha rose, and putting out both her hands, grasped Devon's warmly. "Do feel free to come and visit often—or as often as our charming invalid can see her way to spare you from the sickbed," she added. "I confess I have taken quite a liking to you, Devon. I suppose it is because you are a gentler version of my own willful daughter. Or perhaps because I myself was much the same way in my youth."

Devon left Morehouse in a warm glow of contentment, feeling a fond regard for Agatha. She suspected that the woman's brusque manner hid a feeling of loneliness and she resolved to visit her again at the first opportunity. Though nothing had been said, she knew that Agatha Moreland would be a friend, and she was thankful for the opportunity to become better acquainted with her.

As she walked back to Hawkshead, her own increasingly impossible situation receded in importance and it was not so imperative that she make plans to leave at once, to remove herself from the sight of Gareth Davencourt, before she became more involved.

As she reflected later, it was unfortunate that she did not go forward with her plans to leave Hawkshead at the first opportunity, for within the next few weeks, she was plunged into a nightmare of fear from which she could not escape.

# CHAPTER SIX

She was to remember the day she began to be really frightened because it began so innocuously in comparison to the horror that was to come later. When she reflected long afterward, she wondered why she had not taken flight immediately. Her only excuse was that she had believed, foolishly, that she was able to protect herself. A stupid rationalization, she realized later, but by the time she was forced to admit that the situation had gone beyond maliciousness, and had become actively dangerous, it was too late for escape, even if she had wanted to flee.

The incident in the woods, where she had known such fear, coupled with the destruction of her room, and the earlier, unproved, episode of the stone globe crashing down on her, combined to make her admit that someone was doing his best to frighten her away from Hawkshead. But she stubbornly refused to leave; there must be some reason, she told herself over and over again, for such actions against her, and she was determined to discover the reason. And not only the reason, she told herself firmly, she would also learn who was responsible.

Gareth had called her to the library the day after the incident in the woods. He and several of his men had searched the woods for clues, but though they had found slight evidence, in the form of broken branches and blurred footprints, they had not been able to discover anything further. When he suggested that perhaps she had been mistaken—perhaps the man had indeed been a poacher in search of illegal game—she had agreed reluctantly, since he seemed so willing to dismiss the incident in such a manner. But though she had agreed outwardly, she knew that this was not the

case. The shadowy figure who had sought her out among the dark
shelter of the trees had not been the product of her imagination,
and he had not been in search of illegal game. He had been after
her. And the next time—if there was a next time—she would be
ready for him.

But even her stubborn determination left her unprepared for
events that had been building, unknown to her, since her arrival
at Hawkshead. Had she known that subsequent events would
place her own life in jeopardy, she might have abandoned her
pride and run from Hawkshead to safety.

✻❖✻

Lady Davencourt had requested some new embroidery silks,
and Devon had volunteered to walk to the village for them. It had
been so long since she had been out, she thought the air might do
her good.

She put on her stoutest walking boots, for the weather had
thawed just enough to make walking difficult, and the ruts in the
road were too slushy to walk in. But the air had the fresh smell of
spring on the way, and she breathed in deeply as she walked
along, not minding the occasional slip and slide as her foot met a
hazardous patch of half-frozen ice.

She had tucked a letter to Cecily in her pocket, thinking she
mustn't forget to post it. Not that it held anything of importance,
she though wryly. How could she explain to her sister her feelings
for the Master of Hawkshead, when she couldn't explain them
satisfactorily to herself? As yet, she had made no mention to
Cecily of returning home, although she knew she mustn't procras-
tinate much longer.

She walked along and found her thoughts occupied with Lady
Elinor and Lord Davencourt. Elinor had become a frequent visitor to Hawkshead, and Devon had seen Lady Elinor and Gareth
walking the grounds deep in conversation, seemingly unaware of
the cold. Every time she saw them together, a spasm of nameless
pain caused her to wince and turn away, and she knew it would
not be long before they announced their marriage plans. Indeed,
she could not understand why they had not had the marriage bans
called; if she was correct in her assumption concerning Lady

Elinor, each day that went by would be more difficult to explain. She wondered, too, at the grim expression Lord Davencourt now habitually wore, and at his increasing thinness. Lady Elinor also was showing the effects of some inner conflict; she seemed taut and nervous, her beauty subdued by a brittleness that seemed about to crack under tension. It was all very puzzling.

Her purchase of the silks completed and the letter posted, Devon hurried back to Hawkshead. The air had turned colder, and clouds massing in the distance promised another snow; she wanted to reach the safety of the house before the storm hit. The first flakes of snow were falling as she pulled open the front door. She hurried to Lady Davencourt's room and the comfort of the fire.

When she was admitted to Leticia's room, she was thanked warmly for the silks and pressed to take tea.

"You look chilled, my dear," Lady Davencourt said with concern, handing her a steaming cup. "Do sit by the fire."

Leticia poured fresh tea for herself, then asked casually, "Have you seen Kit? She seems to have disappeared."

Devon glanced around the room. Kit was not in evidence and she was surprised. The little white cat was a constant companion of her mistress and usually resided in Leticia's lap or at the foot of the bed.

Devon volunteered to search, but Leticia said she expected Kit was not too far away; it was just unlike her to be absent for such a long time.

"Lady Elinor visited while you were in the village," Lady Davencourt told her conversationally. "She did not stay long; her manner was distraught and when she found Gareth was not here, she came to see me briefly. I have never seen her so agitated. She mentioned your name, Devon, in the most peculiar way." Leticia paused and glanced at Devon.

"Lady Elinor mentioned me?" Devon asked after a moment's silence.

"Hm . . . yes." Leticia seemed to be wondering whether or not to tell her what Lady Elinor had said, and unaccountably Devon felt uneasy.

At last Leticia said, "Elinor said the most ridiculous thing—she said she thought you were in love with Gareth! Imagine! Well, of course, I assured her that was absolute nonsense . . ."

Lady Davencourt trilled on, watching Devon carefully, but Devon ceased to listen. She had talked with Lady Elinor but twice since the Christmas ball, and Gareth's name had not been mentioned either time. She could not understand how Lady Elinor had made such a disastrous deduction. She was horrified. She believed Lady Elinor would not stop at anything in her goal of marrying Gareth, and Devon did not want to take the chance of being exposed in her folly. She could just imagine the mockery in Gareth's eyes if Lady Elinor told him of her belief that Devon was in love with him. It would be unendurable.

What was Leticia saying? She wrenched her thoughts away from her problem in time to hear ". . . but of course I said I would not dismiss you."

"Dismiss me? Lady Elinor asked you to dismiss me?" Devon echoed somewhat stupidly.

"Yes, my dear. Weren't you listening? She was so upset. Flinging accusations. Well, when I told her I simply would not believe such a thing, she became almost hysterical in her denunciation of you. She said she would find a way. Whatever that means. I told her she must calm herself—her behavior was bordering on . . . well, I needn't go on. I suggest you forget the whole thing; perhaps I shouldn't have mentioned it, but I was so surprised at her outburst. I confess she left me quite exhausted." Leticia sighed and lay back among the pillows on the couch.

Concerned, Devon asked, "Can I do anything? Get you something? You look quite pale."

"No, my dear. I think I shall just rest this afternoon. Such an excess of emotion seems to have tired me more than I realized."

Devon brought a knitted shawl and covered Leticia, saying awkwardly, "Lady Davencourt, I don't know what to say."

"Say nothing, my dear. But I would advise you to keep out of Elinor's way. She has a most appalling tendency toward vindictiveness."

"Yes, Lady Davencourt—and thank you."

Leticia's eyes closed tiredly, and Devon left the room, quietly closing the door.

She stood in the hall for a moment, trying to catch her breath. So, Lady Elinor had pressed Leticia for her dismissal, she thought angrily. But why? Surely Lady Elinor could not possibly think . . . no, it was too absurd. Lady Elinor was a woman who was supremely confident in her power over men; it would not occur to her that any woman would provide competition—of any sort. Well, Devon would never know the reason, since she would be leaving as soon as possible.

She was so shaken at Leticia's conversation, she failed to wonder why Leticia had mentioned it at all. Reasons and explanations—and warnings about the conduct of someone of Elinor Chadmoore's stature—were certainly not discussed in front of servants, even "upper" servants such as she. Had she stopped to think, she might have wondered at such a flagrant breach of propriety from a woman who had been raised to believe in, and who supported, these rules of conduct.

She could not know at the time, but she had made a dangerous error in underestimating the importance of Leticia's confidences.

She crossed to her room, thinking she would sit down immediately and write to Cecily informing her of her decision to return home until she could secure another post.

As she set about gathering her writing materials, she happened to glance at the bed. Why, there's Kit, she thought in surprise, seeing a white ball of fur in the middle of her bed.

"You naughty cat—don't you know your mistress has been looking for you?" she scolded in mock anger as she went to the bed. She reached down to pick up the little cat and recoiled in speechless horror.

Blank, staring eyes met hers as she looked down. The little cat was dead, stabbed through the heart with a pair of scissors. As Devon stood in frozen disbelief, a drop of blood welled from the wound and slid down the white fur, staining the coverlet. One little paw was thrown out, as if in supplication, and its mouth was opened in a grimace of soundless pain.

She stared at the little cat, remembering the times it had jumped into her lap, purring, or darted under her skirts to play hide and seek. The grotesque object on the bed did not resemble the little cat she had been so fond of, and she felt a scream rising in her throat as her mind attempted to deny the evidence of her eyes. She backed away from the bed, one hand raised in front of her as if to ward off the horrible sight.

She felt the doorknob pressing into her back as she unknowingly retreated to the door. The solid wood against her shoulders broke her hypnotic gaze and she found herself running down the hall blindly. She raced down the stairs, her only thought to find Gareth and tell him of this monstrous deed.

She threw open the doors of the drawing room and looked about wildly. He was not there. She continued down the hall and burst through the doors of the library.

Gareth was standing by the window. At her unceremonious entrance he turned and said in astonishment, "What . . . ?"

But Devon flung herself into his arms, sobbing and pointing frantically toward the door. He held her for a moment until her wild sobbing ceased, then gently held her away from him and asked, "Devon, what is it? Is something the matter with Leticia? What has happened?"

She could only shake her head, and he said more firmly, "Devon, sit down. You must compose yourself and tell me what is wrong."

He led her to the couch and shouted for Jergens. When the butler hurried into the room, Gareth curtly ordered brandy and Jergens returned almost immediately with a decanter.

"Can I do anything, my lord?" Jergens asked, his normally dignified expression slightly shaken at seeing Devon in such distress.

"No. I can handle this. Do not say anything to the servants; I want to find out what has happened first. You may go."

Gareth sat beside her and offered his handkerchief. She wiped her eyes, sobbing convulsively again, and he pressed a glass into her hand.

"Drink this," he ordered.

The brandy burned her throat and she coughed, but it seemed to calm her somewhat. She became aware of the concern in his eyes and made an effort to speak.

"I'm sorry. I don't usually become hysterical," she gulped, twisting the handkerchief into a ball.

"What happened? I have never seen you so upset."

"The cat . . ."

"What cat?"

"Kit—Lady Davencourt's cat." She couldn't bring herself to say the words. Obediently, she sipped at the glass he held to her lips again and drew a shaky breath.

"Now. What about the cat? Come, tell me." He cupped his hand under her chin, forcing her to look at him. "Tell me," he repeated gently.

"I . . . she . . ." Devon stammered, then continued in a stronger tone, "I found Kit on my bed. Lady Davencourt said she was missing, and all the time she was lying dead on my bed!"

She knew she was not making sense, but couldn't make the effort to explain further. She looked at Gareth helplessly.

Lord Davencourt was obviously making an effort to understand what had happened; in a puzzled tone he repeated, "Dead?"

"Someone stabbed her." Tears filled her eyes again and she drew a shuddering breath. "Whoever it was put her on my bed; I just found her there. It was horrible. Horrible!"

"Wait here. Drink some more of this brandy; it will help steady you."

He left the library and she heard him call for Jergens. She waited nervously, jumping when a log fell from the fire. In a few moments, Gareth returned.

"Jergens is disposing of . . . the body. I think you should go to your room and lie down for a while. I will have to tell Leticia."

She shivered at the mention of returning to her room, certain that the vision of the little body on the bed would haunt her. Gareth noticed her reluctance and said, "On second thought, stay here. I will have one of the servants bring a blanket and build up the fire. Don't worry—I will get to the bottom of this," he added reassuringly.

He went upstairs again, and a few moments later, Devon heard Leticia scream. She started to get up, thinking to go to Leticia and comfort her, but the brandy was having a strange effect on her. She sank back onto the couch again and thought she would just wait a few moments until the room stopped spinning. She would go to see Lady Davencourt when she didn't feel so drowsy.

Dimly, she heard running footsteps and then the front door slammed. A horse galloped down the drive, but she was too sleepy to wonder about it.

✻⇔✻

When she woke, the library was dark except for the dim light from the fire. She wondered why she was here, and then remembering, shivered.

The house was quiet and she wondered what time it was. She stirred under the blanket someone had put over her and immediately Gareth was bending over her. She was surprised that he would be here, instead of with Leticia, and sleepily she asked, "Gareth?"

He sat on the edge of the couch and reached for her hand. "It's all right, Devon. The doctor came and gave Leticia a sedative. He looked in on you, and since you were sleeping so soundly, thought that would be the best medicine."

"How . . . how is Lady Davencourt?" she asked, wondering why it was so difficult to concentrate on what she wanted to say. Her head ached and her mouth felt dry; it seemed as though her tongue could not form the words.

"I'm afraid the shock was too much for her; she has had a slight relapse," he answered gravely.

"Oh dear, poor woman." Her concern for Leticia, and then the brutality of what had happened, cleared her mind somewhat and she tightened her hold on his hand when she asked, "Gareth, who would do such a thing to a defenseless creature? It's so senseless." The use of his name came easily to her lips, and she knew that was how she had been thinking of him—as Gareth, not Lord Davencourt. It seemed comforting to her at the moment.

"I don't know. I shall set about trying to clear up the mystery, but first I wanted to make certain you were all right."

"I feel fine now. I can't understand why I slept so soundly though. Perhaps the brandy . . ."

Gareth laughed softly. "That wasn't brandy, Devon. In his agitation, Jergens took the wrong bottle—he gave you some of my best whiskey, which is quite a bit stronger than brandy. I forgave him his error when I saw what a calming effect it had on you."

He smiled, then added, almost to himself, "I shall have to remember that."

She smiled drowsily back at him and closed her heavy eyes. A long time later, she started awake briefly and sleepily noted that Gareth still sat beside her. She went to sleep again, comforted by the expression of tenderness softening his hard features as he looked down at her.

*⁂*

Dr. Norris came again the next day to examine Leticia and directly afterward was closeted in the library with Lord Davencourt for some time.

Devon had tried to see Lady Davencourt that morning, but was met at Leticia's door by the stone-faced Mrs. Murphy, who refused her admittance. When Devon had wanted to know why she couldn't see Lady Davencourt and had pressed the woman for an explanation, Mrs. Murphy had looked at her coldly and said, "Haven't you done enough?" before closing the door firmly in Devon's face.

There was nothing to do but wait to talk to the doctor. She hovered unobtrusively, she hoped, by the stairway, waiting for him to emerge after his consultation with Lord Davencourt. She hoped Dr. Norris would tell her of Leticia's condition and thought he might be able to suggest anything special she could do for the sick woman.

At last she heard the murmur of voices in the library cease, and the doctor opened the door saying, "So, Gareth, I don't think it's anything serious—but with her past history, I think we should be careful."

He closed the door and started down the hall where Devon met him and introduced herself: "I'm Devon Brandwyne, Doctor, and I wonder if I may take a few moments of your time?"

"Oh, so you're the little lady who found the cat," Dr. Norris said. "Terrible business. Don't know what's happening to people nowadays."

He cupped her chin in his plump little hand and turned her head back and forth, examining her face with bright blue eyes.

"You don't look much the worse for your experience," he said critically. He sighed wistfully, "Ah, the resilience of youth!"

"Thank you for your concern, Doctor, but I'm fine. I wanted to ask you about Lady Davencourt."

"Hm . . . yes. Well, Leticia does not have a strong constitution —I'm afraid this little incident was a bit much for her to handle. But she'll be fine soon. I wouldn't worry, my dear." He squeezed her arm and winked reassuringly.

"Doctor, what I meant was—is there anything I can do to help her?"

"Gareth is going to talk to you about that." He looked over his shoulder and added, "I think he would like to speak to you now."

She followed the doctor's glance and saw Lord Davencourt standing by the library door. He nodded and stepped inside.

"You go on, my dear. I'll see myself out," Dr. Norris said briskly, slapping his hat on his round, balding head and walking to the door.

❈✿❈

Gareth absently offered her some sherry, which she declined, then said without preamble, "Dr. Norris has decided Lady Davencourt should have complete rest for a time. This experience has affected her adversely, and he is afraid of a relapse."

He paused for a moment and drank deeply from the glass he was holding before continuing. "He thinks the situation is serious enough to warrant the engaging of a nurse, but fortunately, Lady Davencourt's personal maid has had some little experience in nursing; she will be able to look after Leticia competently, I think."

Lord Davencourt sat on the corner of his desk, one booted foot swinging negligently, and stared at her when he had finished speaking. His scrutiny made her nervous and she clenched her hands in the folds of her skirts, hoping he wouldn't notice. Unfortunately, the gesture was not lost on him and he smiled slightly in that mocking way she resented.

After a short silence, when he seemed to be waiting for her to speak, she said faintly, "Then you will have no need of my services; I have no nursing experience. I will pack and be ready tomorrow, if you will be so kind to arrange for a conveyance to take me to the nearest station."

She looked up at him, hoping the tremble on her lips was not noticeable, and when he remained silent, she was at a loss, not knowing what it was that he expected of her. He seemed to be engaged in some inner struggle, but she was scarcely aware of that in trying to overcome her own inner conflict. This was the opportunity she had been waiting for; she could leave now without having to give tiresome explanations about why she wanted to quit this post.

No one would question her sudden departure in view of the circumstances of Leticia's illness and her own lack of nursing experience; no one would ever know how disastrously she had nearly made a fool of herself by falling in love with Gareth Davencourt. The situation had been solved to her best advantage, and she knew she should be thankful. It was absurd that she should feel such pain at the thought of leaving.

Lord Davencourt had come to his own decision while she was wrestling with her thoughts. Still frowning, he said, "There will be no need for you to pack. Dr. Norris was most complimentary about your effect on Leticia until this unexpected setback. He indicated that prior to the . . . incident . . . Leticia had improved tremendously, and he felt it was due in large measure to you."

"That was kind of him," she managed to say.

He continued as if he hadn't heard her, "The good doctor also feels that it will benefit Leticia for you to remain—to provide some company for her—quietly, of course. And only for a few hours a day."

Boldly, she asked, "And I take it you are not in agreement with Dr. Norris' advice?"

"Do not put words into my mouth, Miss Brandwyne," he snapped. "If the doctor feels this is the best way, then—we shall follow his instructions."

"Then I am to stay?" she asked, not knowing whether she wanted his answer in the affirmative or not.

"I thought that was understood. Isn't that what we have been talking about? You seem inattentive, Miss Brandwyne," he said, frowning more blackly than before.

Her uncertain temper, which she had been trying to hold in check during this last exchange, threatened to snap. Stiff-lipped, she said, "It is not that I am inattentive, Lord Davencourt, but your words seem to be at odds with your expression. I cannot tell whether you wish me to remain or not."

"Damn it! It is not for you to interpret my expression!"

"Oh, I see," she interrupted swiftly, caution flying to the winds as her temper rose, "it is only for the Master of Hawkshead to interpret the expression and emotions of others!"

For a moment she thought he would strike her in his anger and she knew she had gone too far. His face turned scarlet with the effort to control himself and it was his turn to clench and unclench his fists. She watched him anxiously, and after a few moments was amazed to see his face clear as he gave a shout of laughter.

"You are incredible, Miss Brandwyne! No one else would dare to talk to me like that, and I must say it's damned amusing to hear it from a snippet of a girl."

He laughed again at her astonished expression and his eyes danced as he said, "I did not know we were harboring a bluestocking."

"I am not a bluestocking," she replied indignantly. "I simply refuse to be treated in such a cavalier fashion by a man who is too proud and arrogant . . ."

She was interrupted by another roar of laughter. "You had better look to your own defenses in that regard, Miss Brandwyne. I have never met such a stiff-necked, evil-tempered woman in my . . ."

"Lord Davencourt, I did not come here to trade insults with you," she said chokingly.

He held up his hand as if in protest. "Quite right. I apologize again," he said, in a tone that indicated he meant no such thing.

He checked his amusement with an effort and said, "Then I trust you are agreeable to remaining with us for a while longer?"

"Well . . . yes. For a time—but only as long as I am needed," she conceded reluctantly.

Suddenly serious, he replied cryptically, "I think we have needed you all along, and never knew it until now."

Her heart gave a lurch at his words; was it possible that he was actually saying that he himself needed her? She clutched at the thought greedily; how she had changed, that a few words could become such a treasure! She wondered briefly if such moments were all she could expect, and then her mind was filled with only one thought—she was going to stay!

Bemusedly, she went to the door and climbed the stairs to her room. She forgot her decision to be away before the marriage of Gareth and Lady Elinor; forgot her resolution to leave Hawkshead before she became more involved with Gareth.

A tiny, insistent voice inside her warned that staying would be foolish, that she would only be hurt, but she brushed aside these warnings in her elation. She was going to stay!

*❋⟡❋*

It wasn't until a few hours later, while she was reading contentedly by the fire in her room, that it suddenly occurred to her to wonder about poor Kit.

She had been so shaken by what had happened and then later so preoccupied with Lady Davencourt and her own decision about whether or not to leave, that she had forgotten about the unfortunate little cat.

Frowning, she tried to reconstruct the events leading to the discovery of the cat in her room. Fragments of Lady Davencourt's conversation came back to her: ". . . became almost hysterical in her denunciation of you . . ." and ". . . she would find a way . . ." and still, ". . . tendency toward vindictiveness . . ."

So, Lady Elinor had been in the house that day—and from Leticia's own account had been upset and hysterical. Was it possible that Lady Elinor was responsible for the death of Kit? No, it was too absurd. Even if Lady Elinor hated her, why should she choose such an appalling method of frightening her away when all she had to do was tell Gareth and he would dismiss her?

Another thought came to her. She remembered wondering whether Lady Elinor had been the person who came into her room and wreaked such havoc there. She had been suspicious of her at the time, but dismissed the thought as unreasonable. Now she wasn't so certain.

But—wait. If Lady Elinor was responsible for trying to frighten her away from Hawkshead, who, then, had followed her in the woods?

Lady Elinor had not been seen in the house that day, and Foxgrove was several miles from Hawkshead. Gareth had found no hoofprints in the snow, and it was ludicrous to assume the fastidious Lady Elinor had walked to the house, lurked about in the woods to frighten her, and had walked back to Foxgrove when the mission was accomplished.

Though she had outwardly agreed with Lord Davencourt that the person who had followed her that night had been a poacher, she realized now that she had agreed to please him. She should have insisted that whoever had sought her in the woods that night had done so for a purpose, and that purpose was to frighten her away.

Finding the cat in her room had been a grisly attempt at a more sinister threat; was it a macabre symbol of what would happen to her if she refused to heed the warning? Or was it simply the product of an unbalanced mind? Whatever it was, the situation was far more dangerous than she had feared. She *must* discover who was responsible for this hideous act.

Mrs. Murphy's face swam before her eyes. Could she be the person responsible? She had been here all three times the unsolved incidents had taken place. She considered the housekeeper briefly, knowing that for some reason Mrs. Murphy disliked her. Shaking her head, she dismissed the woman, realizing that the housekeeper would never do anything to harm Lady Davencourt in any way. And she would certainly not kill Leticia's cat for any reason, knowing how fond Lady Davencourt had been of Kit.

Her head ached from her speculations and she admitted wearily she was no closer than before to solving the mystery. Perhaps the only thing she could do was remain on guard and hope something would come to light that would help her come to a conclusion. A very unsatisfactory solution, she thought, and tried not to feel uneasy.

# CHAPTER SEVEN

When Devon was finally given permission to see Lady Davencourt two days later, she was shocked at the change in the woman. Leticia had always been pale, but her complexion had been the translucent paleness of the delicate-skinned. Today her face was pasty-white, with eyes shadowed by huge purple circles. Her hands lay on the brightly knitted shawl the maid had put there, perhaps in the hope of adding a cheery note in the darkened room, but Leticia's nervous fingers plucked at the threads as if to pull them apart.

She was dressed in a colorful bed jacket of pink and blue, but unfortunately this only served to accentuate her extreme pallor and Devon was alarmed as much at this, as at the listlessness of Lady Davencourt's greeting.

Forcing herself to act normally, Devon said cheerfully, "The doctor said I'm only to stay for a short while; we mustn't tire you. You have only to conserve your strength and in no time you will be up and about."

Lady Davencourt looked at her wanly and said nothing.

Feeling somewhat at a loss, Devon asked, "Would you like me to read to you?"

As if she hadn't heard, Leticia turned burning eyes on Devon and said urgently, "Who would do such a thing? My poor little Kit never harmed anyone. Anyone!"

Before Devon could answer, Lady Davencourt burst into tears and Devon rushed to the bedside and put her arms around the woman. Murmuring comfort, she smoothed Leticia's hair with one hand and patted her hand with the other, but Lady Davencourt twisted away and lay with her face to the pillow.

In desperation, Devon said, "I know Lord Davencourt will make every effort to find out what happened, and punish the person responsible. I know that is not much comfort, but there is not much more he can do."

"Do you think he will really be able to find out who committed this grisly act? Oh, Devon—I would feel so much better if he did!"

"Of course, he will. You mustn't worry about it. You must concentrate on regaining your strength."

Mary came in at that point with a steaming cup of tea for the sick woman, and Devon took her leave, saying she would be back the next day. Lady Davencourt nodded and took Devon's hand, pressing it weakly. "You are such a comfort, Devon dear. I don't know what I would do without you. I'm so happy you came to Hawkshead."

✳︎☙✳︎

Lucy met Devon in the hall and told her that Courtney Chadmoore was waiting in the drawing room.

"Lucy, you should call Lord Davencourt. What have I to do with Mr. Chadmoore?" Devon replied to the girl's statement that Courtney was waiting to talk to her.

"But, miss. I told him I would find the Master—he said it was you he came to see."

Now what was Courtney about, Devon thought irritably, as she went down the stairs and into the drawing room where Courtney was standing.

"Courtney, I've told you . . ."

"Yes, yes. I know. I wanted to see whether you were all right."

"All right? Of course I am," Devon replied crossly, thinking that Courtney was the last person in the world to whom she would confide her fears.

"Oh," he said, obviously puzzled. "I thought that after your terrible experience the other day . . . it must have been quite a shock."

"How did you know about that?" she demanded.

"Gareth stopped at Foxgrove this morning to talk with Elinor. She was so upset at the story, she had to tell me. So, I came to find out how you were."

Devon wondered just why Elinor was so upset—could it be because her scheme had failed? She said calmly, "I have recovered, thank you. But perhaps you should be asking after Lady Davencourt. She has had a slight relapse after Lord Davencourt told her about Kit."

"Yes, so he mentioned. Has anyone discovered who is responsible?"

Devon hesitated before replying. "No. I presume Lord Davencourt is making inquiries, but I have not been told if he has made any progress. Perhaps in view of Lady Davencourt's illness, it might be best . . ."

"Surely you cannot be saying that it would be best to forget about it?" Courtney asked incredulously.

"Well, I think she has been upset about the incident more than we realize, and perhaps it would be best for her not to pursue any inquiries," she answered carefully.

"But, Devon, hasn't it occurred to you that your finding the cat in your room might be some sort of attack on you?"

"Courtney, you are talking nonsense. Who would want to attack me?" she answered curtly, unwilling to let him know she had been having thoughts along the same line herself.

Courtney said uncertainly, "Then why do you suppose you found the cat, and that it was killed in such a disgusting manner . . ."

"Courtney, I refuse to discuss it further. When Lord Davencourt finds out who is responsible, we shall know the answers. Until then, any speculations we might make will be utterly useless," she said more briskly than she felt. "Unless, you have some information of your own?"

"Devon!" Courtney exclaimed, shocked.

"Never mind. I was only trying to engage your attention elsewhere than on this morbid discussion. I confess the thought of that poor little cat is making me queasy."

Instantly contrite, Courtney said, "Perhaps you would like to take a drive with me to take your mind away from this unsavory subject?" His eyes started to sparkle at the prospect of squiring Devon, and he continued encouragingly, "I have just purchased a new harness mare from Gareth, and I would like to know what you think of her."

The thought of taking a drive, as well as the idea of trying out a new horse, was irresistible to her and she accepted eagerly, to Courtney's pleased amusement.

A few moments later they were in the stable yard where Courtney had left his horse and trap in the care of one of the grooms. Devon admired the sleekly shining chestnut mare with the delicate blaze decorating her finely chiseled head and after Courtney had assisted her into the trap and climbed in himself, he handed her the reins.

"Oh, Courtney—may I?" Devon asked delightedly.

"Of course. I could see you were eager to try her for yourself," he replied teasingly.

They left the yard at a smart trot, Devon handling the high-stepping mare with ease. They flashed past the gates, which stood open during the day, and Devon waved at the gatekeeper, who sat huddled by his small stove in the tiny gatehouse.

Devon put the willing mare through her paces as they continued down the road, and at last reluctantly slowed her to a walk.

"Oh, Courtney!" she exclaimed. "She handles perfectly. She is a beautiful animal!"

"I thought you would enjoy her," he responded, taking the reins from her hands. "But then, Gareth doesn't waste his time with anything but the finest."

She nodded absently, her eyes taking in every detail of the animal in front of her.

Courtney asked, "How did you come by your skill with horses, Devon? The ladies of my acquantance have not had such a fondness for the beasts, and seem content to make do with hacks."

"My father taught me to love horses. Before he . . . died . . . he had quite a stable, and even dabbled in breeding. Of course, not on as grand a scale as Lord Davencourt, but he did manage to produce a few horses that were enviously looked upon by his friends." She laughed, in an attempt to ignore the lump in her throat as she thought of her father, and continued, "He gave me my first pony when I was three years old, and ever since then I have appreciated good horseflesh."

"I daresay you graduated from your pony eventually?"

"Oh yes, by the time I was eight he put me on one of his Thoroughbreds. A gentle mare that I egotistically thought was beneath my advanced capabilities. She soon abused me of that idea as I promptly fell off." She laughed again at the memory and Courtney joined her.

"So then what happened?"

"Well, I was so angry that I had made a fool of myself that I insisted on riding that mare every day until I could handle her with some degree of competence."

"So even at that tender age you had a mind of your own?" Courtney teased.

She started to deny this, but then ruefully had to agree. "It was fortunate that I did, because soon after that my father insisted that I accompany him to the hunt. I hated the idea of riding to hounds—I always secretly hoped the fox would escape—but I did enjoy the excitement of taking fences at such speed."

She hesitated, then said, "I think my father always wished he had had a boy who could share these things with him. Perhaps that was why he taught me so much about horses—I was the next best choice."

"Well, all I can say is—I'm glad your father did not have a boy. I am quite satisfied with the female he managed."

She started to reply, but at that moment Gareth appeared cantering down the road toward them. He reined in his horse when he drew near, and said, "Well, Miss Brandwyne. Courtney. Isn't it a trifle chilly to be taking a pleasure drive?"

Courtney answered smoothly, as if unaware of the black frown on Gareth's face, "I just wanted Miss Brandwyne to have a look at the new mare I bought from you, Gareth."

"And what does Miss Brandwyne think of her?" Gareth asked coldly.

Refusing to be referred to in the third person, Devon answered for herself, "I think she is a lovely mare, Lord Davencourt. She has obviously been well trained, for she responds to the lightest touch on the reins. A truly fine animal."

"I am glad you approve of my training methods, Miss Brandwyne," Gareth answered mockingly, glaring down at her.

Courtney began to protest Gareth's contemptuous attitude, but Devon put a restraining hand on his arm and he subsided unwillingly. This gesture was not lost on Gareth, for he tightened his lips, and with a curt good-by, spurred his startled horse and galloped away down the road.

They sat in silence for several minutes, the pleasure of their outing lost after the meeting with Lord Davencourt; then Courtney said lightly, "Gareth can be a bit overbearing at times. I wouldn't let it upset you, Devon."

"It's all right, Courtney. But I think I should be getting back now."

Courtney obediently turned the horse around and they rode back to Hawkshead silently. When they pulled into the stable yard, Gareth was not in sight, and Devon breathed a sign of relief. She thanked Courtney for the ride and as he helped her from the trap, he gave her hand a comforting squeeze.

She smiled at his concern for her and said, "Don't worry about me, Courtney. And thank you again for the ride."

"Any time you want to borrow her, Devon, you have only to ask. That goes for me too." Courtney smiled in his teasing manner, but underneath the banter of words, she could tell he was more serious than she wanted him to be.

# CHAPTER EIGHT

Devon was sitting in the drawing room, reading, when she heard carriage wheels on the drive. She glanced out the window and was surprised to see Lady Elinor and Courtney stepping down from the carriage.

Lady Elinor was obviously in a temper about something; she brushed by Courtney's extended hand with an impatient movement and swept up the curved stairs to the door, an angry frown distorting her perfect features.

Devon thought it best if she retreated before Lady Elinor came into the house. She started quickly down the hall, hoping to reach the stairs before Jergens opened the door. The butler was in the act of doing so when the great door was flung open in his face, barely missing his nose.

Lady Elinor stood on the threshold for a moment, but when Jergens recovered his customary dignity and stepped forward, she brushed by him as if he did not exist. She spied Devon, who stood frozen on the bottom stair, shocked into immobility by this display of excessive rudeness.

Lady Elinor advanced toward Devon, her eyes glittering with hatred. Courtney came up from behind and put a restraining hand on her arm, saying, "Elinor—have you lost your senses?"

Elinor jerked away and addressed Devon in a soft tone vibrating with malice, "So, here you are. I ought to scratch out those green eyes, which seem to have inspired such misplaced devotion! Oh, you were not content to entrap Courtney with that innocent expression, you mealy-mouthed, sniveling creature. Oh no—you had to . . ."

"Elinor!" Courtney cried in desperation. "Please, Devon, pay no heed—she is not herself!"

"I need you to make no excuses for me, Cousin!" Elinor hissed, never taking her eyes from Devon's unbelieving face.

"You, with your sneaking, guileless ways," the woman spat the words at her. "Well, my dear Miss Brandwyne, you do not have the ammunition to compete with me! I . . ."

"Lady Chadmoore," Devon interrupted, at last finding her tongue in the face of such an unexpected attack, "I do not know what you are talking about. I think you must be unwell to come bursting in, in such an ill-bred manner. I do not have to listen to you. Now if you will excuse me?" Devon turned and started up the stairs, trying to control the trembling that was threatening to overtake her in her fury.

"Elinor!" Courtney cried again, desperately trying to restrain the enraged woman. But Elinor shoved Courtney to one side and raced up the stairs after Devon.

Devon turned to see what the commotion was about—Courtney had fallen heavily against one of the chairs in the hall, and there was a sickening sound of splintering wood—Lady Elinor reached her and sank her long fingernails into Devon's arm.

Devon cried out in pain and tried to wrench free. She looked into the maddened eyes of Elinor Chadmoore and felt real fear rising in her. In that moment, she realized what a fool she had been to underestimate this woman. She knew beyond a certainty that Elinor was dangerous and in desperation, she jerked her arm free. The motion sent her spinning into the balustrade, and for an instant she half hung over the rail, grabbing frantically at air. Her clutching hands found the banister at last and she gripped it tightly, closing her eyes thankfully.

A sudden clattering sound opened them again and she stared transfixed at Lady Elinor for a moment. When Devon had pulled free of her grasp, Elinor had lost her balance also, and was teetering on the stairs, arms wildly flailing.

Devon shoved herself away from the banister and made a frantic attempt to catch Elinor as she fell. But her fingers slid uselessly along the smooth satin of Elinor's gown, and Elinor tumbled down the stairs, falling in a disordered heap at the foot of the stairway. She lay there, unmoving.

For a moment everyone was frozen in horror, looking at the huddled shape of the woman lying grotesquely on the floor. Jergens stood bent over Courtney, one arm reached out to help him up; Courtney held one hand to his head, from which blood dripped, and one arm lifted to grasp the butler's hand; Devon leaned awkwardly against the railing, her knuckles showing whitely as they gripped the wood for balance.

Time seemed to stand still; no one had the power to move until the front door crashed open for a second time and Gareth stood framed in the doorway. He took in the frozen tableau in one glance, and as his eye fell on the motionless Elinor, strode quickly across the entry, bellowing for someone to fetch the doctor. He whipped off his cloak and covered Lady Elinor with it, glancing up at Devon and ordering curtly, "Find Mrs. Murphy. Have her ready one of the upstairs rooms at once."

Devon started to hurry off, released from her frozen stance by the authoritative command in his voice. There would be time for explanations later, her numbed mind told her; the important thing right now was to make Elinor as comfortable as possible. Oh God, she thought desperately, don't let her die!

Courtney at last managed to regain his feet. Leaning heavily on Jergens' arm, he limped over to where Gareth knelt beside the unconscious Elinor. Gareth looked up at him with an unfathomable expression in his dark eyes and said abruptly, "Jergens, help Mr. Chadmoore to the library and give him some brandy; he looks as though he's going to collapse. And have one of the maids bring a towel for that gash. The doctor will see to him after he has attended Lady Elinor."

*✳✿✳*

Devon paced the floor of her room, rubbing her arm where angry bruises were already forming. She had seen the doctor arrive and bustle hurriedly into the house from the side door. His horse and gig had stood in the courtyard for a full hour now, and Devon wondered frantically what was taking so long. Her imagination pictured Lady Elinor dying of her injuries, and she had to force her thoughts away from this gruesome speculation.

She could stand the inactivity no longer; she slipped from her room and started downstairs. Courtney was standing in the entry, a bandage wrapped around his fair head.

"Courtney! Are you all right?" she asked in concern.

"Yes. Just think what a dashing figure I will cut around town, with a piratical, romantic scar on my forehead," he replied in a teasing manner.

"A scar? Oh no! How can you be so complacent about it?"

"Serves me right; I should have been more forceful in restraining Elinor."

"How . . . how is she?"

"The doctor seems to think she will recover; only bruises and a bump on the head."

"Thank heavens!"

"But—there have been other . . . ah . . . complications, and the doctor advises that she remain here for a time."

"Here—at Hawkshead?"

"I can understand your reluctance to be in the same house with her, Devon, especially after what happened, but . . ."

"It's not that exactly . . ."

Gareth's voice broke in on their conversation and both of them turned toward him guiltily, each for a different reason. They spoke simultaneously:

"Gareth, I'm sorry to have caused . . ."

"Lord Davencourt, please let me explain . . ."

Grimly, Gareth held up a hand to silence their respective outbursts. "Courtney, a room has been prepared for you; I suggest you retire early. Miss Brandwyne, there has been enough confusion for this day; please go to your room also."

Devon exclaimed angrily, unwilling to be dismissed in this abrupt manner before she had a chance to explain, but he anticipated her protests and continued authoritatively, "We will discuss it later."

She went furiously back to her room. How dare he treat her in such a fashion! But she calmed herself with an effort, remembering Lord Davencourt's strained face and shadowed eyes, and thought that he was just as upset—probably more so, she conceded grimly—as she about the accident, and his abrupt manner was just an outlet for the anxiety he felt about Lady Elinor.

Feeling somewhat better after this rationalization, she wandered aimlessly about the room until a sudden thought struck her: what had Courtney said? Something about—oh yes, further complications hindering Lady Elinor's recovery. Now what did he mean by that, she wondered curiously.

When Lucy brought her dinner tray, Devon winced at the girl's goggling expression. She had forgotten by now the servants would know more about the situation than she herself did, but she refrained from any remark that might be repeated in hushed tones later in the servants' hall. She said calmly, "Just put the tray on the table, Lucy; that will be all."

Lucy crossed the room, glancing back at Devon several times. Carefully, the girl put the tray down and made several meticulous adjustments with the silver. Devon waited impatiently; the girl was obviously stalling for some reason, but Devon was not in the mood for any discussion about the incident. She repeated, "That will be all, Lucy."

Lucy turned, opened her mouth as if to say something, but at Devon's expression, bobbed a quick curtsy and scuttled out of the room, giving Devon a wide berth.

What was that about, Devon wondered irritably; she looked as though I might bite her! She forced herself to put Lucy from her mind as she sat down to her dinner, but several minutes later, after pushing her food around the plate, she realized she was too tired and too upset to eat anything. She covered the tray with her napkin and tumbled into bed to sleep restlessly, chased by nightmares through the night.

***

The following morning was bleak and cold—like my mood, she thought as she pushed aside the draperies. Dark forbidding clouds were massing in the distance and there was a smell of rain in the air. As she stood at her window a jagged thread of lightning flashed through the clouds and she could hear the distant mutter of thunder. Appropriate for the day, she thought bitterly, not knowing how right she was.

Mrs. Murphy met her in the hall as she was going to see Lady Davencourt and the housekeeper coldly told her that Leticia had been given a sedative and the doctor did not wish her to be disturbed, as she had been greatly upset by the news of Lady Elinor's accident. Devon was disturbed herself at the look of contempt on the housekeeper's face and asked her if anything was the matter. She was startled by the vehemence of the woman's answer.

"Miss Brandwyne, don't you think you have caused enough trouble here? I think it would be better for all of us if you were to go away and leave us in peace," the woman hissed at her. "Everything was going so smoothly before you came—with your sly ways, trying to gain the Master's attention."

"Mrs. Murphy, what are you talking about?"

"You know well enough, miss. First, there was the upset in your room—which still has not been explained. Then there was your insistence that someone was following you in the woods, when no one has been able to find any evidence. And finally, Lady Davencourt's cat—which *you* found in your room and profess to know nothing about. Oh, you're a sly little baggage—I knew that from the moment I set eyes on you."

"Mrs. Murphy, I refuse to stand here and listen to your oblique insinuations. Are you suggesting that I planned all these things? Because if you are, I can assure you . . ."

"It's not my place to suggest anything," the woman said coldly, "but there are some of us that do think it strange that these unexplained incidents have happened only to you—and that there has never been any evidence to suggest that you are telling the truth."

"Mrs. Murphy!" Devon exclaimed, shocked at the housekeeper's disdainful attitude.

"And I don't want you bothering the Mistress. First the shock about her cat, and then finding that the Lady Chadmoore had an accident at your hands was almost too much for her. You stay away from her—do you hear?" And with that last threatening note, the housekeeper disappeared into Leticia's room leaving a stunned Devon to contemplate the firmly closed door.

She was still standing there when Courtney came out of his room at the end of the hall. He was fully dressed, with a cloak hung over his arm. The white bandage sat incongruously upon his fair head, but Devon did not smile when she saw his expression.

"Devon, I must talk to you," he said, as he came up to where she was standing.

"Yes, Courtney. I wanted to talk to you, too, but perhaps now is not the time."

"It is urgent, Devon. Is there someplace we can talk privately?"

Devon considered. "Well, perhaps the drawing room. I do not think we can be overheard there."

Courtney carefully closed the drawing room doors and guided Devon to the couch after making certain they were alone. She began to be frightened at his furtive manner and asked, "Courtney, what is the matter? Why is everyone acting so strangely? You said Lady Elinor is going to be all right—you did tell me the truth, didn't you?" She heard the rising note of fear in her voice as the possibility of a serious injury to Lady Elinor rose to haunt her.

"Yes, yes. Elinor is all right," Courtney assured her, and she took a shaky breath in relief. But his next words alarmed her even more when he asked, "Devon, you didn't push her down the stairs, did you?"

She could feel the blood rushing from her head as the enormity of the question came to her. Her mouth became so dry she could not speak—only sat there dumbly, looking at him as he moved jerkily about the room.

"Confound it! I did not mean to ask you that. I know you didn't push her. I'm sorry, Devon—it's just that I'm so upset I don't know what I'm saying." He sat beside her and reached for her hand, which she snatched away before he could touch it.

"Courtney! You don't think that I . . . ? That I could . . . ?" She swallowed hard and forced herself to continue, "Is that why everyone has been avoiding me? Because they think I could deliberately try to injure Lady Elinor? Is that what they all believe—even Lord Davencourt? Courtney, answer me!"

"Elinor told the doctor you pushed her. She . . ."

"But why? Why would she say that?" Devon interrupted frantically.

"She said you were jealous . . ."

"Jealous! Of whom?" The absurdity of the accusation angered Devon and her fear receded momentarily, to be brought back in a rush as Courtney answered.

"Jealous of her—and Gareth. She was saying all sorts of things —that you are in love with Gareth, and that when you found out they were to be married, you took the first opportunity to be rid of her . . ."

Devon forced herself to ask, "And was Gar—Lord Davencourt present when she made these accusations?"

"Yes."

The single word tolled like a funeral bell in her mind and she thought surely she would faint if she heard any more, but Courtney pressed on, inexorably. "She said the reason she came to Hawkshead yesterday was in response to your note, in which you said you would do anything to stop the marriage and threatened her in . . ."

In her horror at what was happening, she barely heard his words, but her consciousness grasped at what he was saying finally, and she asked, "Note? What note?"

Puzzled at her uncomprehending expression, Courtney replied, "Why, the note you sent yesterday by way of Mrs. Murphy. Don't you remember?"

"I never sent any such message," she replied, more shaken than before. "And I certainly would not send any notes with Mrs. Murphy; why, she and I hardly speak!"

"But, Devon," Courtney returned, his puzzlement increasing at her vehement denial, "I saw it myself."

"Then let me see this missive I was supposed to have sent. Have you got it with you?"

Courtney hesitated. She repeated, "Let me see it for myself."

"Elinor was so angry, she tore it into little pieces and threw it on the fire," he admitted finally, miserably.

"What!"

"I'm sorry, Devon."

She felt blackness closing in on her and knew she was going to faint. With an effort, she forced herself to take a deep breath and the buzzing in her ears faded. Her only thought now was to prove that Lady Elinor was lying about being pushed down the stairs. She couldn't do anything about the missing note, so she would have to approach this nightmare from the only way available to her—prove the fall was an accident. But how? How?

A thought came to her and she cried, "Courtney, you were there! You saw what happened on the stairs. You can vouch for the fact that I did not push Lady Elinor!"

Courtney's expression became even more bleak as he looked away from her eager face and stared silently at the floor.

"Courtney—what is the matter? Why do you hesitate?" she asked frantically.

"I'm sorry, Devon," Courtney apologized again.

"What? What do you mean?"

"I . . . I didn't see what happened. Elinor pushed me out of the way as she went up the stairs. I fell against the chair and must have blacked out for a few minutes. When I came to, all I saw was Elinor falling. I'm sorry, Devon . . ." he faltered miserably.

Desperately, she forced her mind to seize upon another possibility. "Then—Jergens! Jergens was there too!" Her spirits lifted again as she thought of the butler.

"No, Devon. I've already asked him. He says he didn't see what happened either. He was trying to help me and was turned away from the stairs."

"Oh no!"

She sat stunned as the seriousness of the matter overwhelmed her. Who would believe her, Devon, if Lady Elinor persisted in this insane accusation? Even Courtney had his doubts. As for Gareth; she shuddered and forced herself not to think of Gareth. Why should he believe her when Lady Elinor insisted that she had received a note from her, and then when she came to Hawkshead to confront her, Devon had pushed her down the stairs in a frenzy of jealousy?

Courtney's voice broke in on her misery. "Devon, I have to go back to Foxgrove now. I'm sorry, my dear, to leave at such a time, but I must. If you need me, send one of the lads with a message, and I'll come immediately. All right?" He patted her numb hand awkwardly. "All right?"

She nodded dumbly, hardly aware of his departure. She was thinking that once she had seen an injured bird brought home by her father and put into a cage; she felt like that poor bird now, who had beat its wings against the bars of the cage in its terror and fright, seeking escape. Miserably, she covered her face with her hands, her mind blank with despair.

# CHAPTER NINE

Devon knew she could not just sit by and allow Lady Elinor to make such a falsely vicious accusation, yet she shrank from visiting the woman personally, remembering the hatred she had seen in Lady Elinor's eyes.

She moved numbly through the next two days, keeping to her room, as she couldn't bear the thought of seeing the accusation that she knew would be on everyone's face. The doctor came and went several times and she could only hope Lady Elinor was recovering from her fall.

Hopefully, she waited for the summons from Lord Davencourt that she had been certain would come immediately, and when it did not, she thought that he must surely be convinced of the truth of Lady Elinor's story. This hurt her more than the accusation itself, because she had thought he would at least be fair and give her a chance to explain what had happened.

She toyed with the idea of leaving Hawkshead and going home to Cecily, but she knew she could never leave until her innocence in the matter had been proven—somehow.

So, she paced the floor of her room with a growing sense of impotence until one day she thought of Agatha Moreland.

Of course! she thought excitedly; Agatha would be able to give her some much needed advice. She remembered Agatha's final words to her the last time they had seen each other, encouraging her to come and visit her. Well, she thought grimly, she would take her up on her offer and go today.

✳⟨♤⟩✳

She walked briskly, not allowing herself to imagine what the woman would think when she burst in unannounced. But to Devon, caught up in what seemed like a nightmare from which there was no escape, Agatha Moreland's hard common sense seemed like a haven from the confusion that surrounded her, and she was willing to take the risk of being rejected with dispatch after she had reached her destination.

As she approached the front door and raised the knocker, she was certain that she had been presumptuous in calling upon the formidable woman without even having sent a message first, but there was nothing to do but wait to be admitted.

When she was ushered into the august presence, Agatha looked at her calmly and said, "Come in, my dear. I've been expecting you."

"I'm sorry if I have intruded," Devon said as she placed herself in the chair Agatha indicated.

"What nonsense. I told you I wanted you to visit me, and you've come at just the right time," Agatha returned crisply. "Betty has just baked fresh biscuits and now I will have someone to enjoy them with."

They exchanged a few pleasantries while the maid bustled in and out with the tea tray, and when Betty had finally taken herself off, Agatha looked at her piercingly and said, "You do not look well; I think you have lost weight since I last saw you."

"No, Mrs. Moreland, I'm fine," Devon lied, somewhat disconcerted by the woman's acuteness.

"Well, from what I've heard, everything isn't fine. I expect that is why you have come. I've been waiting."

Devon looked startled at this announcement, and Agatha said, as she poured a cup for Devon and passed her the plate of steaming biscuits, "You look surprised, Devon. I may be isolated here at Morehouse, but news does travel; what that arrogant nephew of mine does not tell me, I learn from other sources." She laughed softly. "Betty's niece is a maid at Hawkshead."

"Then I think you must be better informed than I am," Devon

answered with a touch of bitterness. "I have not had the opportunity to talk with Lord Davencourt since Lady Elinor's accident."

"Ah, yes. Elinor's accident," Agatha repeated. "I hear in her spitefulness, she had accused you of engineering the whole thing."

"How did you know that?" Devon asked in surprise.

"Did I not tell you I have my sources?" Agatha said.

She relented at Devon's woebegone expression and said kindly, "Surely, you do not think that anyone believes what Elinor has said about you?"

"Yes, I think they do. Especially Lord Davencourt. He has not even given me an opportunity to explain what happened," she answered painfully.

"Oh pooh. I refuse to discuss such nonsense."

"It is not nonsense to me," Devon said angrily.

"Well, then, you will have to believe me when I say that Gareth does not give credence to Elinor's story."

"How can you be certain?"

Agatha answered impatiently, "Because he told me so himself. But he also informed me of something much more important; something I'm going to tell you at the risk of his displeasure, since I'm not certain that he would want you to know just yet."

It was Devon's turn to be impatient, though she tried to conceal it while Agatha paused to take a sip of tea. She waited while Mrs. Moreland dabbed fastidiously at her lips with her napkin, then smoothed it again on her lap. At last Agatha said, "You knew, of course, that Elinor was pregnant?"

"Why . . ." Devon hesitated, then decided she would have to be honest if she was ever going to get to the bottom of the mess she was in. "I was not certain, though from something Lady Elinor said, I thought it must be so," she admitted. Then, "But what do you mean—was?"

"The fall she took on the stairs caused her to miscarry."

So, Devon thought, this was what Courtney meant by "further complications." No wonder Lady Elinor had been so virulent in her accusations! The loss of the baby must have weakened her hold on Gareth. But why was Agatha telling her this?

"Perhaps you are wondering why I have told you," Agatha commented when Devon remained silent at this latest piece of news.

Surprised at the woman's acuteness, Devon could only nod.

"I suppose Gareth would have preferred to tell you himself—but then, as he so rudely informs me—I am an interfering busybody, and I know that nephew of mine; he probably would not feel it important for you to know right now—and I feel that it is."

"But why? What does that have to do with me?"

"Must you be so obtuse, Devon? Now that Elinor has lost the one thing that could have bound Gareth to her, she will not be content to allow you to escape lightly. Is there some way you can prove you did not push her? For if she decides to have you charged, it won't matter whether Gareth and I stand behind you. Remember, we weren't there."

"Yes," Devon answered bitterly, "and it will be her word against mine, in which case I will certainly lose."

"Is there any proof?" Agatha repeated.

"No. Courtney and Jergens were both there, but Courtney told me neither of them saw exactly what happened. Oh, Agatha—what am I to do?" she cried desperately.

"The first thing to do is keep your wits about you," Agatha replied crisply. "Tell me everything you remember."

So Devon told her the events leading to the nightmarish confrontation on the stairs. She concluded with the mystery of the note she was supposed to have written calling Elinor to Hawkshead.

When she had finished, Agatha sat silently for a time before she asked, "And Courtney said it was Mrs. Murphy who delivered the note?" At Devon's nod, she continued musingly, "That is very strange. Why would Mrs. Murphy deliver such a note in the first place. It would certainly seem that she would give it to one of the stable lads to take. A matter of position, at least, if I know Mrs. Murphy."

Devon sat silently, considering what Agatha had said. She had been so upset when Courtney told her what Elinor was accusing her of, that the fact of how the note was delivered had seemed unimportant at the time. She was wondering how to approach the housekeeper for an explanation when Agatha interrupted her thoughts.

"I think the best thing for you to do is have a talk with Gareth about this supposed message. I don't think Mrs. Murphy would give you any explanation, but if Gareth asked her she will be bound to answer. It seems that you have a most insidious enemy —and I don't think it is Elinor Chadmoore."

Devon could only gape at her, as if Agatha had suddenly lost her mind, or she herself had.

"Why are you staring at me like that, Devon?" Agatha demanded.

Devon found her voice and managed to say, "What do you mean you don't think Lady Elinor is responsible? She was in the house that time my room was destroyed; she was there when Kit was killed! And if that isn't enough, now she is accusing me of deliberately trying to injure her by pushing her down the stairs!"

"Devon, you are becoming overwrought—a most unsuitable condition for a young woman of your good sense. Now is the time to use it, and not become hysterical," Agatha said crisply.

"But . . ."

"Consider this: Elinor Chadmoore has never been subtle. She wouldn't know how to be. A person of her extreme self-confidence and conceit—as well as her somewhat limited intelligence— prefers a direct confrontation. You saw that for yourself the day she came to the house, and then when she insisted loudly that you pushed her." She waited for Devon's reluctant agreement before she continued.

"No, I think, for some reason, she has become a pawn as much as you," she said, looking directly at Devon to determine her reaction. "Someone wants you to think Elinor is responsible for the malicious incidents that have been contrived to frighten you away. The question is who?"

Devon had to admit at least one point in Agatha's argument: Elinor Chadmoore was direct; Devon herself had experienced that frontal attack too many times to doubt the authenticity of it. But was it possible that she and Elinor were being played against each other so that any suspicion would be diverted from the person actually responsible? It seemed incredible, but if Agatha Moreland, who was so astute, believed this, then perhaps she should consider it.

She was still unable to dismiss Lady Elinor from her mind as suspect, but at least the conversation had opened up other possibilities which she hadn't considered, and for this she was grateful to the older woman.

Thanking Agatha for talking to her, she gathered her things together and said she must be getting back to Hawkshead, for she had been gone too long already.

Agatha rose with her and pulled the bell to summon her maid, giving instructions that the trap was to be brought round.

"Oh no, Mrs. Moreland," Devon insisted. "I can easily walk."

"Nonsense. Robbie doesn't have that much to do any more; it will do both him and the horse good to have a little exercise," Agatha replied.

While they were waiting, Agatha patted Devon's arm and said quietly, "I caution you to go carefully, Devon—extremely carefully. I think these attempts have been made merely to frighten you for some reason. If something more serious occurs, go directly to Gareth. Immediately. I cannot caution you too strongly on this."

Devon promised to heed her advice, and as she climbed into the trap, Agatha came close to her and said, "And remember, if you need me for any reason, I am here."

✳❖✳

The sun had set and darkness was closing around them when they started up the long drive to the house. Someone had lit the lamps in the front rooms and what should have been like a welcoming light in the darkness seemed instead to Devon to be two great eyes boring into her. Made uncomfortable by this flight of fancy, she moved unconsciously closer to Robbie, who had maintained a silence on the journey from Morehouse. Devon forced her attention away from the house and said the first thing that came into her mind: "Robbie, I'm sorry you had to bring me all the way back here; I wouldn't have minded walking."

Robbie grunted noncommittally and looked warily at the approaching house. Finally, he said in a gruff voice, " 'Tis not that I mind taking you home, miss. 'Tis yon house I stay away from."

She looked at him in surprise, and though it was too dark now to see his expression, she felt a chill pass through her when he continued as if he had read her mind, " 'Tis evil, miss. The house I mean. Puts me in mind of a great bird—waiting for the kill."

"Robbie," she asked faintly, "why do you say that?"

" 'Tis none of my business, miss, but there's been some funny goings on at that house, and I'd be careful, were I you."

"Funny goings on? What do you mean, Robbie?"

"It's whispered in these parts that the Lord Davencourt's brother was"—he hesitated dramatically—"murdered."

"That's ridiculous, Robbie. Lord Davencourt told me himself that his brother was killed by a horse, trampled to death in a stall."

"That's what he says, miss. Others say it was murder."

Now Devon was becoming angry at the man's insistence that Jeffrey's death was not an accident. She told the man so in no uncertain terms, but Robbie was not to be silenced.

He continued, "It were known in these parts that Jeffrey was not a horseman like his brother. He was almost afraid of the beasts, and so would never have gone into a stall with a horse that was known to be vicious. Ponder that if you will, miss."

She objected swiftly, saying, "But that night he had had too much to drink. I understand that sometimes a man will take false courage in those circumstances."

"Nay, miss. Not Master Jeffrey. There weren't nothing could convince him to go near that devil of a horse—drunk or not."

Feeling that the conversation had taken a turn that was not to her liking, she subsided into silence after his last remark. When they reached the house, she climbed down with a stiff thank you and was about to turn away when he touched her arm and whispered, "Take care, miss. There's evil here; make no mistake about that."

She watched him touch the whip to the pony's flank and stood on the steps while he clattered down the drive, trying to quell the uneasiness that was rising in her as she thought of what Robbie had said about murder. Jeffrey's murder. She told herself she wouldn't believe it—Lord Davencourt had told her himself what had happened that terrible night. It was an accident, that was all. But was it?

Would anyone who was so afraid of horses be tempted to go into a stall with a horse known to be vicious—even under the influence of drink? But he *must* have; why would Lord Davencourt lie about it?

Unless—she stumbled on the step and almost fell as a thought occurred to her—unless Lord Davencourt had avoided the truth because he was trying to protect someone, or was involved himself.

No, she couldn't believe it—wouldn't believe it—of him, she told herself shakily. Robbie must be mistaken; a victim of malicious gossip that had been exaggerated out of proportion to the real incident. That must be the explanation, she reassured herself as she entered the house. For what reason would Gareth have to kill his own brother?

✷⟡✷

That night when Lucy had brought her dinner tray to her room, the girl hesitated after placing it in the customary position. Devon looked at her questioningly; she had hardly spoken two words to the girl since the day of the accident when Lucy had seemed afraid of her.

"Miss?" Lucy spoke softly, twisting the folds of her white apron.

"Yes, Lucy—what is it?" Devon asked without curiosity.

"Miss, I thought you might like to know . . ."

"What?"

"Lady Chadmoore felt well enough to go downstairs for a while today. The doctor says Lady Chadmoore is recovering nicely—his own words, miss," Lucy said in a rush, overcome by her boldness in speaking out.

"Thank you for telling me, Lucy," Devon said, grateful for the girl's confidence.

Lucy curtsied and went to the door. She stopped for a moment and said shyly, "I never thought you pushed Lady Chadmoore down the stairs, miss—and I told them all—yes, I did!" She slipped quickly out the door, her small face bright red after her outburst.

Devon felt tears stinging her eyes at this display of loyalty from an unexpected corner. *At least someone in this house believes me,* she thought defiantly.

✳︎☿✳︎

The next morning she decided she would spend a few minutes with Leticia. She knocked softly on the door and was admitted by Mary, who drew her to one side and whispered that Lady Davencourt was sleeping and that the doctor had decided she should rest as much as possible. Leticia did not know as yet about the extent of Lady Elinor's fall on the stairs and it was hoped that she would not learn of it until she was stronger.

Mary closed the door between Lady Davencourt's bedroom and the sitting room and indicated that Devon might like to join her in the inevitable cup of tea. Devon declined the tea, but seated herself, interested in Mary's air of furtiveness.

The woman poured herself a cup and sat beside her. "Oh, Miss Brandwyne," she began, "it must have been simply awful for you. About Lady Elinor's fall, I mean."

Devon knew the woman was trying to be kind, but she felt she had had enough conversation about the unfortunate incident; she made a dismissive motion which Mary ignored as she continued.

"The doctor called me to help him and you never heard such goings on, I'll tell you. Screaming to high heaven and nothing but a sleeping powder would calm that one. It's a wonder the whole countryside didn't hear her!"

"Mary," Devon interrupted, "if you don't mind, I would prefer not to talk about it."

"Oh yes, I can understand that. I just wanted you to know that I didn't believe a word of what she was saying. And neither did the Master—for it was he who insisted that the doctor give her something to make her sleep."

"Mary, I appreciate your concern, but really, I . . ."

"All right, dear," she said, patting Devon's hand, "I won't say any more about it."

Mary lapsed into a comfortable silence and Devon looked at her consideringly. Finally, she asked, "Mary, were you with the family the night Jeffrey was killed?"

Mary looked startled at the turn in conversation, then unaccountably, her face closed and she became almost remote.

"Well, were you?" Devon pressed.

"Yes, miss. But it's something that is best left alone. Such a terrible thing to happen to the Master."

"Yes," Devon said sympathetically. "I can understand Lord Davencourt's feelings to find that his brother was killed by one of his horses."

"Yes, we were all so shocked when he died. And between you and me, miss—Jeffrey Davencourt was far easier to work for than the present Master. He was so kind, always had a good word for the servants. Then when Master Gareth inherited, things took a turn for the worse. Oh, don't mistake me, miss—Lord Davencourt is fair; never would cheat the staff out of anything. And he has built the place up again. But still, Master Jeffrey could make us all laugh."

Devon was becoming confused as she listened to the woman's musings and she asked hesitantly, "Mary, are you saying that Gareth Davencourt became Master of Hawkshead when his brother died? Was he not the oldest son?"

"Oh, bless you, no," Mary answered, "whatever gave you that idea? Jeffrey was the oldest son, senior to Gareth by three years. Though I must say, it was Gareth who ran the estate, and who built it up after his father ran it into debt. Some said it was a bit too provident that Master Jeffrey should . . . die . . . so that Gareth could take full control."

"But . . . Jeffrey's death was an accident."

"So it was meant to be believed. But there are some who say it was no accident . . ."

Mary lapsed into silence again and Devon thought: here it was again—the inference that Jeffrey's death had been planned, that it was in fact murder. And it seemed plain that there might have been a motive. She knew that Gareth loved Hawkshead; had in fact, spent a great deal of time and energy to make the estate a name to be reckoned with. But had he been so ambitious for Hawkshead that he would kill his own brother to inherit?

She shuddered at the thought and Mary said, hoping to comfort her, "It's best left alone as I said, miss; the official verdict was death by misadventure and that's the way we all have to believe."

Devon nodded absently and scarcely noticed when Mary got up to return to Lady Davencourt, leaving her alone with thoughts that were totally unpleasant.

# CHAPTER TEN

Devon was surprised to find Courtney in the drawing room the next day. She told him she would ask one of the servants to tell Lord Davencourt he was here, but Courtney forestalled her, saying, "I came to see you, Devon."

"Courtney, I've told you I cannot entertain visitors, especially at a time like this."

"I did not come here to be entertained, Devon. I have something to discuss with you."

"Well, all right," she said dubiously, "but not here. I will fetch my cloak and we can take a walk about the gardens."

"Whatever you say," Courtney replied so quietly that she stared curiously at him for a moment before leaving to get her cloak.

They walked in the gardens in silence. Devon glanced at Courtney's profile and thought she had never seen him so serious. He appeared to be thinking deeply about some matter and she respected his wish not to talk.

Finally he spoke. "Devon, will you marry me?"

She looked at him, astonished; her mind could frame no answer before he spoke again. "I know you do not love me, but perhaps in time I can induce you to return some of the feeling I have for you. I have loved you for some time; ever since I first saw you, I think."

"Courtney, I . . ."

"Don't say no, Devon—not right away. I know I spoke suddenly; perhaps you need time to think about it. But not too much time, I implore." He looked at her earnestly, hesitating as if he wanted to say more, but not knowing quite how to say it.

Finally, he made up his mind and took her hand, speaking urgently. "Devon, there is something wrong at Hawkshead; I don't know what it is, but I want to get you away. I have a feeling that something disastrous is about to happen"—he held up his hand to silence her questioning look—"I don't know what it is, but whenever it happens, I don't want you here."

"Courtney, are you trying to alarm me?"

"I don't mean to frighten you, my dear. I just don't want anything to happen to you." He held her hand tightly, imploring her to believe him.

"Courtney, you are talking nonsense," Devon said briskly to quell her rising fear. "What could possibly happen to me here at Hawkshead?"

Courtney opened his mouth to reply, but whatever he had been about to say was interrupted as Gareth appeared, walking toward them.

Courtney politely bowed to Gareth, and presently the two men were engaged in a conversation about a mare Gareth had bought that Courtney was interested in. Devon took her leave, ignoring a beseeching glance that Courtney threw at her over his shoulder, and walked back to the house with a troubled mind.

It was true what Courtney had hinted at, she thought. Hawkshead had become sinister, forbidding. There were too many unsolved mysteries here; too many dangerous undercurrents that were beyond her understanding.

She thought of Courtney's proposal as she went to her room. She knew now that she wasn't in love with him; he could be a very amusing companion, she thought, but was not the man with whom she would be content to spend her life. She supposed that a marriage with Courtney, though never inspiring a grand passion, would be better than a gray existence alone, or in the service of others. Several of the girls in school had made brilliant, if loveless marriages, and had seemed content with their bargain, but Devon knew she could never do the same. It would not be fair to Courtney—or to her—to strike such a bargain, knowing she would be playing on his affection to give her companionship and security. It was unlike her to be so indecisive, but then, she reflected wryly, it was unlike her to fall foolishly in love with a man who was scarcely aware of her existence. No, she had no choice; the next time she saw Courtney, she would tell him that it was impossible for her to marry him.

She awakened from a restless sleep by—what? Some small sound had impinged on her consciousness. The room was dark; little light filtered in from the heavy draperies, so she knew it must be quite late. The house was still, yet she had heard something. There it was again—a rustling sound outside her door, and a faint click as the doorknob was turned.

Fear stabbed through her as she remembered the eerie feeling she had known when someone had followed her in the woods. Perhaps this was the same person and now she had an opportunity to confront him and expose him. She must not ignore this chance—at least it would solve one of the mysteries that surrounded her and provide some tangible evidence.

Ignoring her pounding heart, she slipped from the bed, wincing when the bedstead creaked as it was relieved of her weight. The rustling sound in the hall ceased abruptly, as if the intruder had heard it also and was holding his breath as she was.

She groped in the darkness for her robe lying at the foot of the bed, for she dare not take the time to light a candle, and when her searching hands found the garment she quickly belted it around her as she tiptoed to the door. She stood with her ear pressed to the solid wood of the door and could hear nothing.

Perhaps she had imagined the noise? No, there it was again, someone moving stealthily down the hall. Her hand found the doorknob and she gripped it tightly, turning it slowly so it would not betray her by making any noise. The door opened silently, and she blessed Mrs. Murphy for her efficient housekeeping that did not permit door hinges to go unoiled.

Cautiously, she peered into the hall. It was so dark she could see nothing, yet she knew instinctively she was not alone. She waited for her eyes to adjust themselves to the opaque darkness of the hall and was rewarded when she was able to see a dark formless shape detach itself from the wall and move slowly toward the stairs at the end of the hall.

She followed it, keeping close to the wall itself, as if hoping that it would offer some measure of protection. She berated herself for forgetting to bring some kind of weapon, a fire tong, a candlestick, anything—but it was too late to go back now. She knew she must catch this intruder once and for all, because she was sure that he was responsible for the mysterious things that had happened to her since her arrival at Hawkshead.

When she reached the head of the stairs, she saw the black shape disappearing around the corner at the foot of the stairs. She hurried down the steps, certain that the intruder intended to leave by one of the side doors. She had no intention of following him onto the grounds where the trees offered him some measure of self-protection; she must confront him before he left the house.

The light was slightly better on the ground floor, since the great front windows were undraped and watery light from the moon shone weakly on the parqueted floor. She hastened around the corner, intent only upon seizing the intruder, when out of the corner of her eye, she saw an upraised gloved hand wielding a heavy brass candlestick. She tried to twist out of the way, raising her hands instinctively to protect herself.

But as the candlestick came down on the side of her head, her last sight was of two eyes glittering with hatred from under a hood that shadowed the rest of the face. Bright lights exploded in her head and she fell forward into unconsciousness.

# CHAPTER ELEVEN

Dimly, she heard voices buzzing in her ear; the sound was an irritant to her aching head and she moved slightly. Instantly, the voices stopped and she sank into the silence again, vaguely wondering why the floor was so soft and warm. When next she woke, it was to find that she was in her own bed, covered warmly by the covers, which had been drawn up to her chin. The room was dim, but she could see the faint light of dawn showing through the curtains. Another glance toward the side of her bed revealed the small figure of Lucy, wrapped in a quilt. Somehow the sight of the little maid comforted her, and she drifted off again.

The throbbing in her head woke her a second time, and as she put her hand to her aching temple, Lucy instantly was beside her with a glass of water, which she pressed to Devon's lips and encouraged her to drink. Obediently, Devon opened her mouth and drank.

"Thank God," Lucy said gratefully. "Oh, miss, we've been so worried about you!"

Groggily, Devon tried to focus her attention on the wavering figure of the maid. Something was wrong with her eyes—everything was blurred. She opened and closed them several times and even this slight effort caused the pain in her head to increase. Finally, with an effort, she opened her eyes wide, and Lucy's concerned face swam into view.

"Are you all right, miss?" Lucy asked anxiously. "I better call the Master; he wanted to know the minute you woke up."

She turned to go to the door, but Devon said faintly, "No, wait a minute, Lucy. I'm all right—just a little dizzy."

Lucy hurried back to the bedside and helped Devon to a sitting position, plumping the pillows in back of her for support. "And it's no wonder, miss, with that blow on the head. We all thought for sure . . . well, we all thought . . ." Lucy faltered to a stop. "Well, miss, it's been two days, you know, and we've been so worried."

"Two days!"

"Yes," the little maid nodded vigorously, as if to assure Devon of the authenticity of her statement. "Two days since the Master found you at the foot of the stairs. Fair out of his mind he was too," she added wonderingly. "Woke the whole house with his shouting. He even had one of the grooms take his very own horse to fetch the doctor. And nothing would do but that he himself must carry you up the stairs."

Devon wondered briefly how Lord Davencourt had managed to come upon the scene so quickly, but her musings were cut short as Lucy continued.

"We were all in a tizzy, I can tell you, miss. And when the doctor came and shook his head over you, in that way he has, we all thought the Master would bring the roof down with his shouting that he, the doctor I mean, had better make you well, or the Master would see that he would never treat anyone again. Such goings on!" Lucy shook her head, still marveling at the scene.

Devon tried not to shudder when she asked, "Was Lord Davencourt in time to catch the intruder?" for she remembered the horror of that upraised arm she had seen for an instant, and the two eyes glittering in a mask of hatred.

Lucy's eyes widened when she answered, "That's the strange thing about it, miss. There wasn't anyone around—just you lying on the floor beside that candlestick. The Master fair turned the house upside down, but we found nothing. And now, miss, I think you should rest and I will get the Master; I know he is anxious to find out how you are."

A few minutes later, there was a knock on her door, and when she gave permission to enter, Lord Davencourt came in. She watched him as he approached the bedside, and was surprised to see the strain evident on his face; his eyes were shadowed and new lines had appeared at the sides of his mouth, as if anxiety had etched them there against his will.

Despite the throbbing in her head, her heart gave a treacherous lurch as he bent over her and she hid behind a mask of cheerfulness to cover the emotion she felt when he took her hand and inquired how she was feeling.

"Well, aside from the fact that my head feels as though it were about to fly off, I think I am recovered," she said, unable to take her eyes from the face which expressed such concern.

There was a sudden tension in him that she did not understand, and to break the uncomfortable silence, she asked, "Did you discover anything about the intruder?"

"No," he said shortly, "but I did want to ask you what in the name of blazes you thought you were doing trying to catch him by yourself. Will you never learn?"

Now he was angry with her again and she could feel her own temper rising in response to his. "I wanted to find out who he was —to prove that he was responsible for the mysterious things that have been happening." The reasoning that had led her into the hall after the intruder, and which she had been convinced was the only thing to do at the time, now seemed weak in her own ears and she subsided uncomfortably.

Lord Davencourt agreed with her, for he said, "And I suppose you thought to overpower him with your bare hands? That was a stupid thing to do, as you are now aware. You are only fortunate that you were not killed in your folly."

Miserably, she had to agree with him, but her pride forced her to return, "And now that I think about it—how did you happen upon the scene so quickly?"

His eyes narrowed furiously, but he replied, "My dear Miss Brandwyne, did it occur to you that the noise you made when you fell, as well as the candlestick hitting the floor, was enough to wake the dead?"

"Well, no one else seems to have heard it," she replied defensively.

"No one else was on the first floor in the library. But this is ridiculous—surely you are not accusing me of attacking you?"

His sudden question startled her, for she had to admit to herself that the idea had occurred to her briefly. She hesitated a moment too long in her denial and was surprised when he laughed bitterly.

"I can see that the idea has crossed your mind. Well, perhaps I cannot blame you entirely. But I assure you, it was not I."

"How ridiculous," she said, furious to be caught in such a speculation, "of course, I know it was not you—the person who attacked me was much shorter."

"Which brings us to the point at last—do you have any idea who it might have been?"

"No, it happened too quickly—and of course it was too dark to see anything."

"Of course it was, since you neglected to bring something so simple as a light," he replied caustically.

"Are you laughing at me?" she demanded furiously.

"No. I simply find it difficult to believe that you would venture out into a darkened hall in search of someone whom you had reason to believe intended you harm."

"You don't understand. I . . ."

"No, I don't understand," he thundered. "How could you be so unbelievably stupid to do such a thing—to put yourself into such danger without a thought . . ."

"How dare you!" she sputtered. "How dare you talk to me in this way! I heard something in the hall outside my door; when I opened it, I could see someone moving down the hall. I thought it might be the person who has caused all this trouble, and I followed him hoping to discover who it was. You would have done the same thing!"

"Yes—but with a slight difference," he said acidly. "I might have had a chance against this intruder. You are only a woman."

She put a hand to her aching head; her headache had increased with the force of her emotion and she was feeling dizzy again, but she refused to let him know this. Before he could say anything more, she remembered Agatha's advice about the note she was supposed to have written; suddenly it seemed very important to explain her version of Lady Elinor's accident. Through a gathering haze of pain she said, "There was something else I wanted to talk to you about. I want you to know that Lady Elinor's fall was an accident. I most certainly did not push her. In fact, it was SHE who . . ."

"Good God!" he interrupted incredulously, "you were almost murdered, and now all you can talk about is Elinor's misadventure on the stairs? You are incredible!"

"Lord Davencourt, please—the servants will hear you!"

"Hang the servants—I will shout in my own house if I desire; you are not Mistress of it yet!"

He stopped shouting abruptly and furiously turned from her toward the window. His hands clenched into fists and Devon could see the muscle bunching along his jaw as he tried to control his fury.

"I want to talk about Lady Elinor's misadventure, as you call it, because it is important to me that I am proven innocent of her accusation," she said, more calmly than she felt. The pain in her head was even worse, and it was difficult to concentrate on the conversation, especially since Lord Davencourt had turned to her and was glowering fiercely.

Finally, he said in a carefully controlled voice, "All right; since it is so important to you, we will discuss it—but at a time when you have recovered completely."

"If you insist; but I must ask something of you first."

"Anything," he replied sarcastically, "since you are determined to have your own way no matter what I say."

Ignoring his sarcasm, she said, "Mrs. Murphy was supposed to have delivered a note from me to Lady Elinor, in which I challenged her to a confrontation, or something of that sort. I'm not quite sure, since I never wrote that note. I would like you to question Mrs. Murphy about the matter, if you would."

"Well, certainly," he replied in the same sarcastic tone. "Is there anything else?"

"No," she said in a small voice.

"All right. We will question her together, since it means so much to you—but only when you feel well enough. Agreed?"

"Yes—and thank you, Lord Davencourt."

She watched him as he left the room, shaking his head as if exasperated, but she was too elated that he had agreed to question

Mrs. Murphy to think of anything else; soon she would be able to prove that she had not written the note, and then perhaps the matter would be resolved.

*❋⬦❋*

She remained in bed for the next two days until she could get up without feeling dizzy. When the doctor informed her that apparently there were no ill effects, though she should not exert herself in case of a relapse, she ignored him and eagerly went in search of Lord Davencourt to remind him of his promise to confront the housekeeper. Lucy had told her that Lady Elinor had not left Hawkshead, and she was anxious to prove to the woman that she had not written the message to her.

Lord Davencourt sighed when she asked him if he would talk to Mrs. Murphy, but resignedly called the housekeeper to the library.

"Mrs. Murphy," he began when they had assembled there, "there has been some confusion about the note you were supposed to have delivered from Miss Brandwyne to Lady Elinor. Miss Brandwyne insists that she did not write it. Perhaps you would be good enough to explain?"

Mrs. Murphy stood in front of Lord Davencourt like a stone statue draped in black, with marble hands grimly folded in front of her. She turned to where Devon was standing, waiting eagerly for her response, and Devon was puzzled at the look of enmity on the woman's face.

Mrs. Murphy stared at her for a moment, then said, "I'm afraid I don't understand, Lord Davencourt. Miss Brandwyne handed me the note herself, with explicit instructions that it be delivered to Lady Elinor."

"How can you say that?" Devon cried. "You know I did no such thing!"

"Please, Miss Brandwyne," Lord Davencourt interrupted. "Now, Mrs. Murphy. Are you certain of this? I find it most strange that you insist Miss Brandwyne gave you the note; while she is equally insistent that she did not."

"I'm sorry, Lord Davencourt," Mrs. Murphy replied coolly.

"But she did give me an envelope addressed to Lady Elinor, which I delivered personally."

Devon could not believe this was happening; for a moment, in the face of the woman's stubbornness, she almost believed that she had written the note and that now she was losing her mind. But no—that was ridiculous; she had not even heard of the note until Courtney had mentioned it.

Feeling that she was clutching at straws, she said, "But even if it were so, Mrs. Murphy, why would you deliver it yourself? Would it not have been easier to have one of the stable boys deliver it?"

Mrs. Murphy looked at her pityingly before answering. "Miss Brandwyne, don't you remember we discussed the fact that Foxgrove is on my way when I visit my niece and I said I would be happy to deliver it, since I had to pass by there anyway?"

Devon looked helplessly at Lord Davencourt. He looked back at her with a puzzled frown before turning to the housekeeper and saying, "Mrs. Murphy, I will ask you one more time. Are you certain that Miss Brandwyne gave you a message to take to Lady Elinor?"

The housekeeper straightened indignantly and replied, "Lord Davencourt, I've told you exactly what happened. Perhaps Miss Brandwyne is confused about this, as she seems to be confused about so many things. The incident in her room, for one; the imaginary stalking in the woods, for another. Perhaps she needs to go away for a rest, to sort things out in her mind . . ."

Devon was furious at this oblique attack on her sanity, but before she could say anything, Lord Davencourt cut in swiftly, "That will be all, Mrs. Murphy."

The housekeeper inclined her head graciously and left the room. Devon could not help seeing the look of satisfaction on the woman's face as she shut the door and she had to fight down an impulse to follow the housekeeper and shake her until she was forced to tell the truth.

Instead, she turned to Lord Davencourt and said stiffly, "I don't know why she is lying, but she most certainly is doing so. And I intend to find out why."

"Devon, I think it would be better . . ."

Gareth was interrupted by Lady Elinor's voice, saying languidly, "Gareth, dear, would you help me over to the couch? I find I'm still weak as a kitten."

Both of them turned toward the door and Devon saw Lady Elinor leaning gracefully against the doorjamb. She was wearing a peacock blue morning gown that shimmered in the light, and Devon was forced to admit the woman had never looked more helplessly feminine as she did at that moment. She extended a limp hand in Gareth's direction and he moved immediately to assist her.

When he had helped her to the couch and settled her there, Lady Elinor looked at Devon and said, "I see, Miss Brandwyne, now that your plans have gone awry, you are attempting to extricate yourself by placing blame on Mrs. Murphy. Well, it won't work, my dear, because the fact remains that you pushed me down the stairs. In fact . . ."

Gareth interceded, saying, "Elinor, I don't think this is the time to discuss it."

"On the contrary, Gareth," Lady Elinor disagreed, smiling condescendingly at Devon, "this is exactly the time to discuss the matter. Miss Brandwyne has caused nothing but trouble since she came, and this household will be well rid of her. I'm only surprised that you did not send her away immediately after she attacked me on the stairs."

Devon could contain herself no longer. Not caring what the consequences might be, she said angrily, "Lady Elinor, I will not allow you to spread that lie about me any further. If you will remember, it was you who came rushing into the house screaming accusations, and it was YOU who came up the stairs after me. Perhaps in your state of mind at the time, you cannot remember clearly, but I can, and do—and I find it difficult to believe that any lady of breeding could act so!"

Lady Elinor was so enraged she could only sputter. Devon glanced at Lord Davencourt defiantly and was surprised to find him trying to repress a smile; he succeeded in gaining his composure only when Lady Elinor looked at him and demanded, "Gareth, are you going to allow her to talk to me like that? I've never been so insulted in my life! I demand that you dismiss her at once!"

"Elinor, I will decide how to run my own household, if you don't mind," Gareth replied with icy calm. "I have no intention of dismissing Miss Brandwyne at this time."

For a moment Elinor was shocked into silence at the implication of this statement, and Devon felt a thrill of elation. Lord Davencourt was actually defending her! Could it be . . . ? But she wrenched her thoughts away from such joyful speculation as Lady Elinor rose unsteadily and said as haughtily as she could under the circumstances, "Well, if that is your decision, I refuse to remain under this roof a moment longer. Have the goodness to ready a carriage for me; I am going back to Foxgrove until you regain your senses." And with that, she swept out of the room.

Devon took one look at Gareth's tight face and followed her, forgetting in her astonishment at Lord Davencourt's attitude toward Lady Elinor her own immediate problem of Mrs. Murphy and the note.

# CHAPTER TWELVE

Once again Devon decided to visit Agatha. She had tried to think of a clue that would enable her to solve the mysterious—and now dangerous—happenings at Hawkshead. Her head ached from thoughts chasing round and round and leading nowhere. Perhaps Agatha, with her cool wisdom and sharp common sense would be able to help her find a reason for someone wanting to kill her. There—she had admitted it. Someone wanted her out of the way so badly he would not stop at murder. She was a fool not to have left as soon as the strange occurrences began, but it was no use trying to call back her folly. She would just have to make the best of it somehow.

❋�❋

Agatha received her warmly—until she searched Devon's strained face.

"What is it, Devon?" she asked sharply.

"I don't know quite how to begin, Mrs. Moreland."

"Agatha—you may call me Agatha. And begin at the beginning of course," Agatha said crisply, becoming alarmed at the pallor and thinness of Devon's face, as well as the bruise on her temple, which she had not been successful in hiding completely. She led Devon into her bright sitting room, where a fire blazed cheerfully, and after seating Devon, rang for Betty.

"Betty, bring us some brandy—immediately."

The maid scurried off and returned moments later with a tray. Agatha poured a glass and pushed it into Devon's hand. "Drink this—I find that in moments of stress, it does wonders."

Devon replied with a small attempt at a smile, "Lord Davencourt says the same thing; you are remarkably similar in many ways."

"I'm sure you did not come here to discuss the similarities between myself and my nephew," Agatha said briskly, nevertheless pleased at the comparison.

"No. I think someone is trying to kill me, and I could only think of coming to you for help," Devon said, realizing that she was sounding melodramatic, but knowing no other way of introducing the matter.

"Trying to kill you? How?" Agatha's face showed little emotion, but her voice shook slightly, betraying her agitation.

"The other night I heard someone lurking outside my room; when I foolishly went to investigate, I was hit with a candlestick. I'm afraid I am not a very successful heroine, because the intruder escaped without detection."

Agatha gasped but immediately recovered herself and said, "Things seem to have taken a more serious turn since your last visit. Do you have any idea who it might have been?"

Devon shook her head. "It was too dark, and I think the . . . person . . . wore some kind of garment with a hood attached. I could not see the face—only the eyes." She shuddered at the memory of those horrible eyes.

Agatha asked quickly, "Does Gareth know about this?"

Devon grimaced and answered, "Yes. In fact, it was he who discovered me lying at the foot of the stairs."

"Do you think he has any ideas about who it was?"

"I don't know. We haven't had much opportunity to talk about it. And then, there was the matter of Mrs. Murphy insisting that I gave her the note to Lady Elinor . . ."

"What? Did Gareth question her?"

"Yes. I was present also, and she emphatically states that I gave her a message to take to Lady Elinor."

"Hm . . . I wonder why."

"Yes, so do I. I thought you might be able to shed some light on the situation. I've been thinking about it so much I'm afraid I'm more confused than before."

"I think it would be better for you to stay with me for a time,"

Agatha said. "There are too many things I don't understand, and I would prefer to have you safe with me. At least I know we won't have any midnight guests wandering around with lethal weapons."

"But that won't solve anything, Agatha. I have to know who hates me so much that they would want to kill me. And the only way to find out is to remain at Hawkshead."

"Yes, and perhaps get yourself killed for your pains," Agatha replied sarcastically.

"You would stay, if you were in a similar situation."

"We're not talking about me," Agatha answered with a touch of her old imperiousness. "Now, what I suggest is that you return to Hawkshead, inform Gareth that you are staying with me for a time, and see what he thinks of the idea. Perhaps he will have a plan of his own, in which case I will agree to whatever he suggests. Does that suit you?"

※❖※

Gareth stood by the fireplace when she entered the library and she was reminded of their first meeting. He had the same angry intensity burning in his eyes, and the same impatient tenseness in his lean body. But instead of the nervousness she had felt that first night, now she could feel her own anger rising—as it did whenever he looked this way: as though he could not hide his impatience to be rid of her and be about more important matters.

"I wanted to talk with you, Miss Brandwyne. I sent for you earlier, but it seems no one could find you. How in blazes could you go off at a time like this?" he snapped at her, glowering.

"I merely went to visit your aunt, Lord Davencourt. I did not know I was confined to the house," she replied, unable to keep a trace of sarcasm from her voice.

"Don't be ridiculous. Of course you are not confined to the house. But when you disappeared, and no one knew where you were . . . never mind. The point is that you are here now. I wanted to tell you that I have found no trace of the person who attacked you the other night. The servants have been questioned, and all can account for themselves. So, we are faced with yet another mystery of which you are the center."

"What are you implying? Do you think I staged all of these things for some unknown reason? Are you trying to tell me that you agree with Mrs. Murphy that . . . that . . . I am 'confused' and do things I don't remember later?"

"Of course not," he replied savagely. "You have the most irritating habit of putting words into my mouth! I certainly did not intend to say that I thought you were responsible."

"Then what are you trying to say?" she asked rashly.

He stared at her for a long moment, then turned toward the window, where dusk was gathering, making huddled shapes of the trees standing outside. The lamplight shone on his rigid back and he stood outlined in the silver of the window, his hands clenched into fists. Devon could see the muscle bunching along his jaw as he controlled his fury, and she longed to go to him and put her arms around him, pleading with him not to be angry with her. Her love for him swept over her, making her lightheaded, and it took all her control to remain seated where she was. Suddenly, she could stand this awful silence no longer. "Lord Davencourt?" she asked softly.

He faced her, and a spasm of pain crossed his features as he looked down at her. "Devon, I do not know why it is that you exasperate me so. I considered myself indifferent to women until you came to Hawkshead. You, with none of the wiles and sly vaporings and flutterings that so characterize the members of your sex . . . your stubbornness and your pride . . . Damn it! What I'm trying to say is that I think you should leave Hawkshead—especially now, after your experience the other night."

He put his hand to his forehead in a gesture of pain and continued, "Go—marry Courtney—do whatever you wish. But leave me in peace!"

Devon leaped to her feet. "What are you saying?" she cried, not believing she had heard correctly.

"So, you do not intend to let me off lightly," he said grimly. "Well, you will not see the day I grovel before any woman. I do not intend to let you make a mockery of me. So—marry that popinjay you are so enamored of . . ."

"Courtney? You think I am in love with Courtney?" She heard her voice rising in anger, but she didn't care. She wanted to goad her fury, for if she did not, she knew she would fling herself into his arms and beg him not to send her away. She rushed on, caught up in a flood of emotion, her stung pride forcing her to ignore the look of pain in Gareth's eyes as she struggled with her own longing to abandon all pretense. If only he had said he loved her! But he had not. No; instead, he had said he wished her to leave. Without thinking, aware only of her own overwhelming sense of loss, she cried, "Agatha was right when she said men were fools! As for me—yes, I will go, and gladly—before I see you married to Elinor Chadmoore!"

She was so furiously angry she could scarcely continue for fear that she would burst into tears of rage and pain. But because she was hurt, she wanted to hurt him also. "Fortunately, Agatha has invited me to stay with her for a time. Because I will not leave until I find out who is so intent on trying to kill me. And if you think *that*, too, is a product of my imagination, then I suppose the only thing that would convince you is my actual murder. I'm not sorry to disallow you that satisfaction!"

She gathered her skirts to go and swept blindly from the room.

*✧*

The next morning she had packed a valise and was ready to leave. She would send for her trunk later because she was too proud to ask Lord Davencourt to have one of the grooms drive her to Morehouse. Now that she had made the decision to leave Hawkshead, she wanted to be away before she had time to change her mind.

The only thing she dreaded was the necessity of explaining to Lady Davencourt that she was leaving. She knew she could not tell Leticia the truth, so she had decided to tell her that Mrs. Moreland had requested her company for a time, and that Lord Davencourt had given her permission to go.

Squaring her shoulders, she knocked on Leticia's door and was admitted by Mary, who looked at her questioningly. Devon ignored Mary's obvious curiosity and went directly into Leticia's bedroom.

Lady Davencourt was lying on the sofa by the fire, wrapped

warmly in quilts, and at Devon's entrance, she put down the book she had been reading and greeted her warmly.

"Devon, how nice to see you. I thought you had deserted me," she said reproachfully, patting the chair beside the sofa.

Devon seated herself and said, "You look much better, Lady Davencourt. I can see the rest the doctor prescribed has done wonders for you."

"Yes. I do feel better—but so bored. I asked for you, but Gareth felt that I should do without company until I recovered." Leticia sighed and looked so forlorn that Devon knew it was going to be more difficult than she expected to tell Leticia she was going away.

"Lady Davencourt, I'm sorry to tell you this, but Lord Davencourt has decided that I'm to go to Morehouse to keep Mrs. Moreland company for a while."

Leticia looked stricken, raising brimming eyes to Devon, who was feeling more wretched by the minute. She said, "Devon, I don't understand. I need you much more than Agatha does. Oh, Devon—you can't leave now!"

"I'm sorry, Lady Davencourt. But look, you have Mary, who will take excellent care of you—much better than I . . ."

"I don't want Mary," Leticia said petulantly. "I want you. You know all the right things to say, and you have a beautiful reading voice, and I'm never bored with you. No! It's impossible. I won't let you go."

"I'll come and visit every day, if you want me to," Devon said desperately, becoming alarmed at Leticia's distress.

Lady Davencourt's eyes narrowed suddenly and she looked at Devon appraisingly. She said softly, "I know why you're leaving, Devon. It's because of the incident the other night, isn't it?"

For some reason, Devon felt chilled at the undertone in Leticia's voice, but she didn't know why. She said, as matter-of-factly as she could, "What do you mean, Lady Davencourt?"

"Oh, I know about that. Everyone tries to protect me, but they are not always successful. I don't blame you if you're leaving because you are frightened. You were very courageous to remain as long as you did."

Mrs. Murphy, Devon thought—Mrs. Murphy had told her

about the intruder in the house. But she had no intention of up-setting Lady Davencourt further, so she said lightly, "That was an accident, Lady Davencourt. A foolish thing on my part."

"Yes," Leticia agreed, nodding thoughtfully. "You are wise to leave Hawkshead, but perhaps you are not going far enough away. Perhaps you should return to your sister."

Devon looked quickly at Leticia's face, but her expression was guarded, and again she felt uneasy. How much did this woman know? Was Leticia warning her to leave before something terrible happened to her? She didn't know, but she had no intention of asking her and perhaps bringing on another relapse. She answered firmly, "Lady Davencourt, I am not returning to my sister. I am going to Morehouse to stay with Mrs. Moreland for a time."

Leticia was silent for a moment, then she said, in the same soft voice, "Yes, I suppose that is the best thing for you to do. Well, Devon, I shall miss you. Do say you will come and see me oc-casionally."

"Yes, of course I will."

"Good. Now will you send Mary to me? I feel so tired."

✳☺✳

Devon was installed in a cozy guest room on the second floor by Agatha herself. The room faced the front of the house and Devon could see Robbie working industriously, turning the dirt in the bare flower beds in preparation for spring planting. She turned away from the window and surveyed the room, where Agatha had tactfully left her alone after making certain that everything was in readiness.

The furnishings were not as grand as those in her former room at Hawkshead, but the warm rosewood tones of the bedstead and matching wardrobe cheered her dismal spirit, as did the colorfully worked quilt that covered the bed. There was a small bookcase built into the wall, and on closer inspection, she saw that it held many of her favorite volumes; she concluded that she and Agatha had similar tastes in literature and she was grateful that she had found such a friend in Gareth's aunt.

When she went down to dinner, she found that Betty had set the table with care. Fine old silver bearing an intricately designed

"M" resided beside delicate china and shining crystal. The silver candelabra shone down on the soft white linen tablecloth and a bowl of white roses was placed in the center of the table.

Agatha came into the dining room as Devon was admiring the table, and the two of them sat down while Betty began serving.

"Agatha, I don't know how to thank you," Devon began.

"Oh, pooh. It will be good for me to have some company," Agatha said, dismissing Devon's attempted thanks. "Besides, I feel so much better having you here where I can keep an eye on you. I confess I was beginning to be concerned about your safety."

Devon smiled at Agatha's offhand manner; she had seen the relief on the woman's face when she had arrived, but she had no intention of probing Agatha's brusqueness, which she knew covered the woman's true feelings. She was too grateful for the closeness that had seemed to spring up between them.

"Now, tell me. What did Gareth have to say?" Agatha asked.

Devon frowned, not wanting to relive the last scene in the library. She was ashamed at the way she had behaved, but she could not rectify it now.

Agatha looked at her piercingly, then smiled her secret smile. "I see it did not go well. Did you two have words again?"

Devon squirmed at the woman's perceptiveness and knew it would be useless to try to evade the issue. She nodded.

Agatha sighed. "Yes, I can see that you did. What happened?"

"Lord Davencourt indicated that he thought I might be imagining things—that he had not found any trace of the person who was in the house that night. I suppose he thought I hit myself over the head with that candlestick just to be dramatic!"

Agatha's lips twitched, but she said severely, "I suppose he was just as frustrated as you that no evidence could be found. You have to admit, it is mystifying."

"He said he questioned all the servants . . ."

"Just the servants?"

Devon looked at her in surprise. "Of course. That is, I . . . he said he questioned the servants. What are you implying?" she finished in confusion.

"Simply that there were other people in the house that night than the servants. If all the windows and doors were locked, then it had to be someone already in the house. Someone who knew the interior so well that he could get away without detection."

Comprehension dawned on Devon; she wondered why she had not thought of that before. What a fool she had been! Slowly, she said, "Lady Elinor was there; Lord Davencourt, Lady Davencourt, and of course, myself."

"And you did not have any clue who it might have been?"

Helplessly, Devon shook her head. "I'm afraid I did not see anything that could help me to identify the person."

"Then we must use our powers of deduction."

Yes, Devon thought—but that was easy to say. Lady Elinor might have had reason to try to kill me, but she had seen for herself how weak Elinor had been that day she had come to the library; she did not think that Elinor would have had the strength to wield that heavy candlestick. She refused to consider Leticia; the woman had been confined to her bed under sedation for several weeks now, and besides—what possible reason would Leticia have to kill her?

Devon thought of the one remaining person who might have a reason. But no—she told herself—she would not believe that of him. Still, if Gareth thought she really had pushed Lady Elinor down the stairs—regardless of what he had told Agatha—and if he thought Devon's jealousy might be dangerous . . . no, she could not force herself to accept that. How could you love someone and then suspect that person of trying to murder you? It was impossible, monstrous!

With her uncanny ability to follow her thoughts, Agatha asked, "Devon, are you in love with Gareth?"

"I . . . no," Devon said firmly, hoping this would satisfy Agatha.

"What proud, stubborn people you and Gareth are!" Agatha exclaimed impatiently. "Can't see the nose in front of your face—either of you."

"What are you talking about? Lord Davencourt is in love with Lady Elinor . . ."

"As you are in love with Courtney?"

"What rubbish! Where did you get that idea?"

"Never mind, miss. Tell me about Courtney."

Devon was becoming irritated with Agatha's curiosity and she snapped, "It is true that Courtney has asked me to marry him, but I've decided to tell him no. Now, does that satisfy you?"

Agatha nodded complacently, unperturbed by Devon's display of temper. Devon, contrite, began to apologize for snapping at her, but Agatha merely said, "It's quite all right, my dear; you've been under quite a strain these past few weeks. However, we seem to be no closer to solving the mystery than we were before. I suggest we retire early; perhaps in the morning we will be able to put our heads together and find the solution."

✳❖✳

The next morning brought Courtney, racing up to the house on his big gray horse. He flung himself out of the saddle, throwing the reins to Robbie, who stood gaping at him. Devon had heard the rapid hoofbeats coming up the drive and had raced to her window to discover who was in such haste. She was just in time to see Courtney dismount, but before she had time to wonder what he was doing here, the whole house was resounding with his beating on the door.

Devon raced down the stairs, hoping to reach him before he disturbed the whole house. She jerked open the front door just as Courtney was about to renew his assault on the knocker. He stared at her wide-eyed, his expression half wild.

"Courtney! What is the matter?"

"Devon, it's really you! Oh, thank God! When they told me you had left Hawkshead, I thought . . . I thought . . ."

Devon pulled Courtney into the house, giving instructions to the still-staring Robbie to take care of Courtney's lathered horse. She led him into the sitting room, where he threw his arms around her and held her so tightly she could hardly breathe.

"Courtney! Let go of me—immediately."

"I'm sorry, Devon," he said, relinquishing his hold on her. "But I'm so glad you are all right."

"Why shouldn't I be?"

"Elinor finally told me about the other night when you were

almost murdered. I had no idea! Then, when I went to Hawkshead to find out if you were safe, Gareth told me you had left. He acted so strangely, I was almost afraid to believe him." Courtney laughed, a high sound without humor that bordered on hysteria. "I finally got it out of him that you were staying with Mrs. Moreland, and I came directly here to see for myself."

"Courtney, you must get hold of yourself," Devon said, pulling him toward a chair and almost pushing him down into it.

Courtney wiped his forehead with a lace-edged handkerchief as he sat down, and unaccountably, Devon wondered why she had ever thought she was in love with this man. She remembered Gareth calling him a fop, and against her will, she had to agree. Still, he was concerned about her, and for that she was grateful.

"I know it's early, but do you think I might have some brandy?" Courtney asked. "Talking to Gareth when he is in a towering rage does something to one's nerves, I'm afraid."

Devon went in search of the brandy, giving Courtney time to collect himself. When she returned, after deliberately taking longer than necessary to gather the decanter and glass, he was sitting calmly, legs fastidiously crossed, in a chair by the fire.

"Is that better?" she asked, after he had taken a long drink.

"Yes. I seem to have made a fool of myself, imagining all sorts of hideous things that could have happened to you. You don't know how glad I am that you finally had sense enough to leave that horrible place."

"Yes, but it still doesn't solve anything," she replied.

"What is there to solve? It is enough that you are safe here, and don't have to worry any more."

He shuddered delicately, and again she was reminded of the contrast between him and Gareth; Gareth would never run away from any problem, even if it meant danger to himself. Forcing her thoughts away from Gareth, she said, "Courtney, I am glad you came. I have something I want to tell you. I'm sorry, but I am going to have to refuse your offer of marriage."

She had tried to tell him gently, and was surprised to see an emotion—was it relief?—crossing his features. She must have been mistaken, because in the next instant he looked so tragic she almost laughed. Forcing herself to keep a straight face, she said, "Courtney, I'm sorry."

"You are refusing me because of Gareth, aren't you? I knew you were in love with him . . ."

"Why does everyone seem to think that I am in love with Lord Davencourt?" she asked irritably. "What nonsense!"

"Is it?" he asked softly, looking at her intensely.

In spite of herself, she felt her face coloring; to cover the telltale stain, she put her hands to her cheeks and Courtney laughed at her discomfort. "Do you think you can hide your true feelings, Devon? No, you are too honest. If a blush doesn't betray you, your eyes will. You have very expressive eyes, my love."

"Courtney, this is a ridiculous conversation. I refuse to discuss it further," she said curtly, to hide her embarrassment.

"Very well, my dear," he agreed with surprising ease. "Well, since the game is lost on my account, I see no reason to prolong my stay in these parts. Perhaps I will go to Paris and try to revive my desolate spirits in the everlasting gaiety that seems to be a French speciality."

Devon laughed. "You seem to have recovered from your rejection easily enough."

"It is but a pose, my dear. You don't know how my heart is breaking under this gay façade."

She walked him to the door where he stood for a moment looking down at her. Then swiftly, he bent and kissed her. "Gareth is a lucky man, if only he would realize it," he murmured. "But I would be careful if I were you, Devon." He was gone before she had a chance to reply to this curious remark.

❋✾❋

Two days went by. Three. Devon felt as though she were living in a void, waiting for something to happen to release her from this emptiness. She felt she had left Hawkshead under a cloud of suspicion, and her straightforward nature would not permit her to leave all the problems she had left there unsolved. She was restless, moving from room to room, unable to settle to anything, until Agatha threw up her hands and ordered her outside to help Robbie in the garden.

She went gladly, eager for something to do, to occupy her mind with thoughts other than those of Gareth and Hawkshead. She put on her oldest dress, tied a shawl about her shoulders, and presented herself to Robbie for instructions.

Robbie reluctantly allowed her to start setting seeds in one section of the garden, giving her so many detailed instructions about the procedure she had to smile. He moved off to another section, muttering under his breath, but she could tell he was pleased that she had offered to help and had accepted his orders so meekly.

As she dug her fingers into the rich earth and carefully placed the seeds in the ground, she forgot about Hawkshead. The sun was warm on her shoulders, and soon she was humming softly, thinking what a beautiful profusion of color there would be when everything was green and flowering. She was so absorbed in her task that she failed to see the little figure of Lucy hurrying toward her until the girl was almost on top of her.

"Lucy!" she exclaimed with pleasure, when she looked up to see the girl standing before her.

Lucy's round face broke into a smile as she curtsied. "Hello, miss," she said shyly.

"Whatever brings you here?" Devon asked, sitting back on her heels and wiping the dirt from her hands.

"I have a message for you," Lucy answered, pulling an envelope from her voluminous apron pocket. She glanced around as if to see whether anyone was near, and then whispered, "From the Master, I was told."

Surprised, Devon took the envelope from her and slipped it into her own pocket without looking at it. Her pulse quickened and she refused to betray her eagerness to read the note from Gareth in front of Lucy. She looked calmly at the girl and had to smile at her obvious disappointment in not being allowed to share in the excitement.

"How is Lady Davencourt, Lucy?" she asked.

"I don't know exactly, miss," the girl replied. "She keeps to her room and I'm not allowed there, but I do know Mary is having a time—the Mistress isn't pleased at anything she does. Mary said if it wasn't that she had to support her parents, she'd leave. I suppose Lady Davencourt misses you, miss. Do you think you could come back?"

Devon shook her head. "No, Lucy. I'm afraid that is impossible."

Lucy sighed. "Then I suppose we will have to just keep out of the Master's way."

"What do you mean?" Devon asked, surprised at the turn in the conversation.

"Oh, miss—ever since you left, the Master has been in one of his black moods. He shouts at the grooms, and"—her eyes widened —"he even sent back the roast the cook fixed the other night, saying it was too tough! You should have seen Cook, all in tears with her apron over her head! The night before he had refused the pudding—and everyone is all in a muddle!"

Devon wanted to laugh at the picture of Lord Davencourt arrogantly refusing the food; Hawkshead was known for the sumptuous meals the cook fixed, and it was generally agreed that the estate had the best kitchen in the area. It was not the cook Gareth was upset over, that she knew for certain. Keeping a straight face, she said, "Lucy, you have to remember that Lord Davencourt has a lot on his mind . . ."

"But, miss—the Master has never been like this before! Even Jergens doesn't know what to do." Lucy shook her head dolefully and rocked back and forth on tiny feet.

"I'm afraid I don't know what to say, Lucy. Perhaps things will take a turn for the better when Lord Davencourt and Lady Elinor marry," Devon said, grimacing at the idea.

"Oh, I don't think they will marry, miss," Lucy said surprisingly. "Lady Elinor rode over to Hawkshead the other day, and they had the most terrible row in the library. Lady Elinor was screaming and shouting, and then she left all in a flurry. The Master came out of the library looking fit to kill—you can be sure we all stayed out of his way after that!"

So, Devon thought—that was the reason for Lord Davencourt's black mood. In spite of herself, she could not help the feeling of elation that rose in her with the news of the terrible quarrel, and she told herself sternly that she should be ashamed. She should be, but she wasn't.

"Well, Lucy," she forced herself to say, "all lovers have a quarrel now and then; it will pass, and then things will go on as before."

Lucy looked doubtful, but she said, "Yes, miss. Well, I had better be getting back. Mrs. Murphy said I was to come and deliver the message and go right back. She'll skin me if I don't leave right now. By, miss—I hope you come and visit soon."

Devon watched Lucy scurry away, then forced herself calmly to finish setting out the seeds she had been planting. When she was finished, she got up, brushed the small pieces of dirt that were clinging to her skirts, and walked sedately into the house. The envelope felt like it was burning a hole in her pocket, so anxious was she to dash up to her room and read the letter inside.

When she reached her room she untied the shawl from around her shoulders, washed the grime from her hands, and sat in the chair by the window. It was ridiculous to become so excited, she scolded herself. The letter was most likely a notification of her dismisal from Hawkshead: Dear Miss Brandwyne, I regret to say that since your services are no longer needed . . . Yes, that was the only possible reason Lord Davencourt would have for writing to her. In which case there was no reason for her heart to be pounding so, she thought disgustedly as she pulled the envelope from her pocket.

Her hands shook slightly as she opened the flap and took out the single thick sheet of paper embossed with the Hawkshead crest. She smoothed the creases out of the paper and read:

Devon—

Meet me at 8:00 P.M. tonight near the black stallion's pasture. I have some news that will interest you. Tell no one, and come alone.

Gareth

Devon stared at the paper for a long time. There was something about the note that bothered her; something wrong that she couldn't put her finger on. Her first reaction after she had read it was one of relief; he had discovered who was trying to force her to leave Hawkshead. But the longer she stared at the letter in her lap, the more she felt it was a trap of some kind.

Subterfuge was not Gareth's way; if he had something to tell her, he would simply ride over to Morehouse and say it openly—not ask her to meet him in a semi-deserted area of the estate. That is, unless—he had been the one who was trying to force her to leave, and now that she had proved so stubborn he had decided to take a more drastic approach. No; she couldn't believe that of him. She knew in her heart that Gareth might be a lot of things, but a murderer he was not.

Absently her finger traced the strokes the pen had made on the paper. She knew she should consult Agatha about the implication of the note, but she was certain that if she did, Agatha would refuse to allow her to keep the rendezvous—or insist on coming with her. Devon had no intention of exposing Agatha to possible danger, and she knew that she must be at Onyx's pasture that night. No, there was no help for it—she would have to lie to Agatha if need be. She was certain that the frightening and dangerous events that had plagued her since her arrival would be explained somehow tonight, and she had no intention of being frightened away this time.

✳❖✳

The afternoon passed in an agony of waiting. A dozen times it was on the tip of her tongue to tell Agatha, but each time she remained stubbornly silent. She found Agatha staring at her with that penetrating glance and struggled to keep her face expressionless, knowing the woman had an uncanny ability to guess her thoughts.

Dinner was an ordeal; Devon forced herself to chat amiably about the garden, the weather—anything that would keep her mind off the meeting with Gareth tonight.

Finally, Agatha said in exasperation, "Devon, what is the matter with you tonight? You are so nervous—I declare I thought you were going to jump out of your chair when Betty dropped that serving spoon!"

"Nothing is wrong, Agatha," Devon answered, forcing herself to meet the other woman's eyes.

"Well, something must be—I have never seen you so pale. And chattering—you never just chatter about nothing! Are you certain you won't tell me?" Agatha asked, eying her shrewdly.

"I suppose it's just the strain of these past few weeks," Devon answered weakly. "I don't feel quite myself tonight. Would you excuse me? I think I'll go to my room early."

She rose and walked around the table, bending to kiss Agatha's cheek. "I'll feel better in the morning," she said.

Agatha patted her hand, then grasped it tightly. "Whatever it is, I hope you won't do anything foolish, my dear," Agatha said, frowning.

Startled at the warning tone in Agatha's voice, Devon stared at her, wondering how much the woman knew—or had guessed, but Agatha's dark eyes were shadowed as she bent to sip her after-dinner coffee, and Devon chose not to press her for an explanation. There would be plenty of time for explanations after the mystery was solved tonight.

Fortunately for her, Agatha was in the habit of retiring to her room to read shortly after the evening meal, so Devon was able to leave the house without having to make any difficult explanations. She left the back way, checking carefully to make certain the latch was off the door so she could get back in without disturbing anyone after her meeting with Lord Davencourt.

※✦※

The moon was rising as she walked hurriedly down the road, a thinly illuminated disk that shone weakly down on her, and she shivered under her thick cloak as shadows along the road seemed to leap out at her in its pale light. The letter crackled in her pocket as she walked, and again she had the feeling that she was foolishly walking into a dangerous situation. If she hadn't been so determined to get to the truth of the matter, she would have been frightened. As it was, she thought wryly, she was simply dreadfully nervous.

When she reached the field at which end Onyx's pasture lay, paused for a moment. The ominous feeling increased. She looked up at the dark sky and saw great clouds moving across the face of the moon. The clouds were bringing the smell of rain, and there was the distant mutter of thunder. A slight breeze sprang up, carrying with it advance notice of the approach of a storm.

Trying to ignore the warnings her mind started to hammer at her, she struggled across the field through the stiff, dead grass and stones that littered the ground. At last she reached the fence, panting slightly from the exertion.

She looked around in the dim light, hoping Lord Davencourt had already arrived. A shadow moved at the corner of the pasture beneath a cluster of trees and she walked along the fence, squinting in order to see more clearly. She reached the gate where she had stood watching the black stallion parading in front of her so many times and glanced around. No one was there; she must have been mistaken.

Feeling more foolish by the minute, she leaned against the fence thinking she would wait ten minutes. If Lord Davencourt had not arrived by that time she would leave; she wasn't about to stand around waiting his pleasure all night, she thought indignantly.

Five minutes passed. Ten minutes, and no sign from Gareth. She could barely make out the hands on her watch: eight-fifteen. That was strange, she thought; Lord Davencourt insisted on punctuality—in himself and others, and now he was fifteen minutes late for a meeting he himself had arranged. Of course, she conceded reluctantly, something could have detained him. Unless he wasn't coming. Or— A sudden thought struck her and she pulled the letter from her pocket, frowning as she tried to read it in the watery moonlight.

The answer hit her like a slap in the face: Lord Davencourt had not written this note! Oh, the heavy black strokes of the pen were there, but it was not his bold, flowing script that she stared at so intently. Whoever had written the message had tried to copy his handwriting—that was plain—but the effect was stilted, so unlike his that she wondered why she had not known it immediately. Whoever had written it had chanced the fact that she had never seen Gareth's handwriting—but he hadn't needed to take that chance, she thought bitterly. Like a complete fool, she had delivered herself neatly into the trap.

The moon was suddenly hidden behind a cloud and she looked up to find that the storm was approaching rapidly. The wind, which had been a gentle breeze up to now increased slightly, whipping the hem of her cloak about her legs; she felt a sudden chill as though something sinister were about to take place. She heard hoofbeats coming across the pasture and turned to see the dark shape of the black stallion looming closer, galloping toward her.

Onyx slid to a stop inches away from the fence and snorted. She could see the whites of his eyes glistening in the intermittent moonlight as he tossed his head nervously. She had never seen him so agitated; the sheen of sweat along his arched neck and dappling his flank indicated that something had upset the huge animal. Tentatively, she reached toward him and he shied away, stamping his feet and laying back his ears as though she were an enemy.

She was surprised; the stallion had never acted this way toward her, had accepted her presence, and even seemed to enjoy having her near the times she had come to see him. Puzzled, she stared at him as he moved restlessly back and forth, then gasped as he wheeled about and turned the other way.

A long welt along his side and another on his neck gleamed redly in the moonlight, and she knew what had caused his agitation. But who—who would take a whip to this highly strung animal? Not Gareth, her mind cried in denial; he had too much respect—and too much admiration for this horse to mistreat him so.

"Who?" she whispered, her eyes fastened on the trembling stallion, completely forgetting in her concern for him the fact that she herself might be in danger.

Suddenly, she realized she was not alone. Whirling around so quickly she almost lost her balance, she faced the same shrouded figure she had seen in the hall that night; the same figure that had tried once before to kill her. Her hand went to her throat in an instinctive gesture, and she had to force down a scream as those two glittering eyes behind the hood stared back at her.

The figure had come upon her when her attention had been focused on Onyx, and the way in which it stood there, unmoving except for the gleam of those horrible eyes, sent terror stabbing through her.

"What do you want?" she croaked. "Who are you?"

# CHAPTER THIRTEEN

Slowly, gloved hands reached up and pulled back the hood. Pale hair shimmered in the wavering moonlight and Devon did not know whether she would laugh hysterically or break into terrified sobs as Leticia Davencourt stood before her.

"Lady Davencourt," she gasped. "What a start you gave me! What are you doing here—you are not well enough to be out on a night like this." She heard herself babbling on as her fright increased. Leticia Davencourt stood silently before her; the now-angered stallion screamed suddenly behind her, and she felt like she was in some kind of horrible nightmare, caught between two opposing forces against which she had no strength.

"I . . . I don't understand," Devon said at last, unable to take her eyes from Leticia's face.

"I didn't think you would, my dear," Leticia said in a soft voice that sent chills racing down Devon's spine. "You are a most stubborn young woman. I could see that I had to take a more drastic —and final—approach to be rid of you." Slowly, Leticia pulled a small pistol from beneath the folds of her cloak and leveled it directly at Devon.

Suddenly the pieces of the puzzle fell into place in Devon's mind. She knew beyond doubt that Leticia had been the perpetrator all along, and knew also, from the glittering, narrowed eyes, that the woman was mad. Through her terror, she realized the only thing she could do was keep Leticia talking; perhaps she could catch her off guard somehow and take the gun away from her. It was a dangerous foolish plan, she thought, but she couldn't think of anything else; it seemed her mind refused to function beyond a primitive level of self-preservation. No one knew she was here, and she was certain that Leticia had arranged things so that no one at Hawkshead knew she was absent from the house.

"So," Devon said, trying to keep her voice from shaking, "it was you the whole time. But why? If you wanted me to leave, you could have simply dismissed me."

Leticia laughed, a high cackling sound that made Devon shiver. "How simple you are, my dear," Leticia said pityingly. "I couldn't dismiss you because then Gareth would have been suspicious."

The illogic of this remark puzzled Devon. "Suspicious? But why?"

"You do your work so well, my dear," Leticia answered, her voice taking on such a sly, oily tone that Devon recoiled in disgust. "In no time at all you had established yourself as in-dispensable—or so Gareth believed. And when he started to fall in love with you, I knew I had to be rid of you. Gareth is mine—and no one is going to take him from me! I plotted and planned to rid myself of that stupid, weak husband of mine just so I could be free to marry Gareth. Nothing will stop me now!"

"Are you saying you arranged Jeffrey's death? But how? He was trampled to death by Onyx."

"Ah, yes. Brilliant, was it not? All I had to do was taunt Jeffrey about being afraid of that horse, until he had to prove to himself —and to his loving wife—that he could overcome his fear. It was simple enough after that."

Leticia gestured toward the stallion, whom Devon could hear moving about behind her. "As you can see, Onyx hates the whip, and in a small stall—well, it was child's play to anger the horse enough to trample my inebriated husband."

Leticia smiled malevolently. "Just as he trampled Jeffrey, so also is he going to do the same to you. No one will question your death when they find you in the pasture. Onyx already has the reputation of a killer; your death will automatically be attributed to him. See—I have already managed to anger him enough to kill."

As if to give credence to her words, the horse screamed again in rage when Leticia moved closer to the fence. He rushed at her, teeth bared, and Leticia moved hastily away.

Devon had listened to this cold recital of Jeffrey's murder in mounting horror, and now she did not doubt that Leticia would not hesitate to kill her just as she had killed Jeffrey. Frantically, her mind searched for something to say to distract the woman from her purpose, but Leticia continued, "I sensed you were a danger to me the first night you arrived. I went to your room while you were sleeping, and looking at you, so young and pretty, I knew I had to get rid of you. I knew the stone globes on the roof were in a state of disrepair, so I suggested that you take a walk on the terrace that afternoon. It was easy enough to wait until you were directly under me; I sent the stone crashing down, but unfortunately you were too quick for me. I realized that I had to use some other method of frightening you, so when it became apparent that you and Elinor detested each other, I searched for a way to make each of you blame the other when things went wrong— thus diverting any suspicion from myself, of course." Leticia laughed gaily, secure in the knowledge that her plan had succeeded.

"So that was why nothing happened to me in the house unless Elinor was there also," Devon said, fascinated in spite of herself by the perverted workings of Leticia's mind.

"Oh yes. It was relatively easy for me to run across the hall and destroy everything I could in your room after Elinor had left the house that day." Leticia's lip curled as she added, "Poor Elinor— always running to Hawkshead in the hope that I would have some little tidbit to tell her about Gareth. How I enjoyed leading her on, making her angry over some imagined slight of his."

"But was it you who followed me that time in the woods? How could you possibly expect that Lady Elinor would be blamed for that? She was nowhere near the house that day!"

"Oh yes, that. A slight miscalculation on my part. I thought I could be rid of you then—but you were too stubborn to be frightened away that easily. That was a stupidity you will soon regret, my dear."

Devon suddenly thought of Kit, the poor little cat she had found dead in her room. She asked faintly, "And Kit . . . ?"

Leticia frowned. "Yes. Kit. I thought after that, sacrificing the cat would be enough to frighten you into leaving. I underestimated you, my dear; a mistake you will pay for dearly."

Devon could not believe she and Leticia were having this conversation. How could Leticia have fooled everyone into thinking she was such an invalid, when all the time she had had the strength and cunning to conceive and carry out her evil plan? Especially since she, Devon, had seen Leticia so many times as the weak and frail woman, bedridden or scarcely able to take a step from her room. The woman must be a consummate actress, she conceded in chagrin. She said, "I still don't understand how you were able to convince even the doctor that you were in ill-health, when all the time you . . ."

Leticia laughed again, preening herself on her cleverness. "What an innocent you are!" she said cunningly. "A little rice powder for a pasty complexion, some shadow for the eyes, a frail delicate look; any woman with the slightest knowledge of her capabilities can make men believe whatever she wishes!"

Devon knew that she could not keep Leticia talking much longer; the woman had a look of impatience about her, as though she were anxious to be done with her. When Leticia gestured toward the gate with the gun in her hand, indicating that Devon should move toward it, she said desperately, "But Lady Elinor— the accident on the stairs . . ."

"You both played into my hands beautifully that day. It was simple enough to have Mrs. Murphy deliver a note in your name —a note stating that you had succeeded in winning Gareth away from her. I knew nothing would infuriate Elinor more; she rushed to Hawkshead to confront you, exactly as I expected her to do. Of course, a little advance planning was necessary to put Elinor in the frame of mind to believe the note, but that was easily accomplished. If Gareth had not become recalcitrant at the last minute and refused to dismiss you, the plan would have worked to perfection. I would have discredited Elinor as the hysterical fool I know her to be, and you would have been safely away from Hawkshead under a cloud of suspicion."

Leticia stopped talking suddenly and lifted her head in a listening attitude. Hope rose briefly in Devon; perhaps someone was coming! She strained frantically to listen also, but the wind had increased in intensity and all she could hear was the whistling sound it made as it rushed through the trees.

Onyx became frantic as Leticia gestured Devon toward the gate again. With the gun pointing steadily at her, there was nothing to do but move in the direction Leticia indicated.

Devon was told to unlatch the gate. She bent shaking fingers to the task. A long length of rope was tied through the gate and then wound around the fence post, with several large knots tying the two ends together. She fumbled with the knotted rope until it finally fell away from the post, but the latch beneath was rusty and Devon could not work it free.

"I can't get it open," she said, struggling with the frozen metal. It was difficult to see in the dark, and the wind whipped her cloak about her, tangling in her arms, making her clumsy. Leticia exclaimed impatiently and Devon felt the hard muzzle of the gun pressed suddenly into her back.

"Then you'll have to climb under the fence," Leticia said coldly. "Hurry and do so."

The gun pressed painfully into her spine and Devon bent to crawl under the fence, eying Leticia on one side and the pawing stallion on the other. She had just decided to abandon her idea of trying to wrest the gun away from Leticia and take her chances with the stallion when a hard voice said:

"Leticia! What do you think you're doing?"

Devon almost fainted with relief as Lord Davencourt stepped out from the shadows underneath the trees and strode toward them. She grasped the fence post weakly and shut her eyes in thankfulness.

Leticia backed away from the fury in Gareth's eyes and cried wildly, "Don't come any closer, Gareth! You can't ruin my plans now—all we have to do is get rid of her, and then we can be married."

"Leticia, what are you talking about? I have no intention of marrying you. Now, give me the gun . . ." He held out his hand coaxingly.

"What do you mean?" Leticia cried, her eyes becoming distended. "I've been waiting all this time—I thought after a decent interval . . . I mean, after Jeffrey's death . . . I did it so we could be free to marry!"

Devon had stood in frozen silence from the moment Gareth had appeared, but she could see that Leticia was beyond all reason now. She couldn't take her eyes from the sight of Leticia's distorted face with its wild eyes and writhing lips. She had the frightening appearance of a caricature; a mad creature who was disintegrating before their eyes. She said softly to Gareth, "Be careful. She is responsible for Jeffrey's death . . ."

Leticia heard her from the depths of her own private hell and turned furiously toward her, the gun wavering back and forth. "How dare you say that! How can you imply that Jeffrey's death was murder. He deserved to die—that sniveling, weak creature who was not a man . . ."

"Leticia," Gareth interrupted, "that's enough. Now give me that gun!" He took one step toward her, holding out his hand again.

Leticia recoiled from his advance, her face suddenly taking on such a malevolent aspect that Devon shuddered. Leticia backed slowly away from Gareth, muttering unintelligibly. Her foot struck a rock and she started to fall, her sudden screams seeming to rend the air insanely. Before either Gareth or Devon could move, the gun went off with a roar and a scarlet streak of light pierced the night. Leticia fell heavily, her head hitting the fence with a sharp crack. Her screaming stopped abruptly and she lay still, her head twisted at an odd angle.

Devon looked at Gareth helplessly and choked back a scream of her own as he groaned and tottered forward, clutching at his chest. As he fell, she saw a glistening red stain blossoming on his shoulder. For a moment, she stood transfixed, caught up in the horror of the past few minutes; everything had taken place so quickly her shocked mind could not comprehend what had happened—she only knew Gareth was injured.

She flung herself toward him. In the fitful moonlight, his face had a gray tinge, and frantically she put her ear to his chest, praying she would hear a heartbeat. Silence. Then—wait! She could hear a faint beat, then another. Thank God he was alive! She reached inside his coat and her fingers came away red with the blood that seemed to be pouring out of his wound. She looked stupidly at her hand glistening scarlet in the moonlight, only dimly aware of the chaos around her. The wind shrieked through the trees, which groaned as their branches were bent double; the stallion neighed shrilly and thudded back and forth along the fence behind her. A sudden mutter of thunder sent the first driving spate of chilling rain down on them.

Without thinking, she threw off her cloak, covering Gareth with it. She began ripping her petticoat into pieces and wadding the material under his coat in an effort to stanch the bleeding. Tearing a long strip of material, she fashioned a rough bandage to hold everything in place as she tried to think what to do next. Her glance fell on Leticia and she got up and went over to where the woman lay. Leticia's face in death was twisted, her mouth opened in a silent scream; a dreadful parody of the little cat she had killed. Devon turned away, sickened.

She knew she had to get help quickly or Lord Davencourt would die. Already the blood was soaking through the bandage she had made, and she knew he would soon bleed to death if the wound was not treated in a more professional manner.

She considered, forcing her numbed mind to go over the possibilities. Hawkshead was closest, but it would take her a good half hour to make her way there on foot in the rain and the darkness, even using the short-cut through the woods. And in that time Gareth might die. She looked at the stallion, who stood fairly quietly now, trembling in the aftermath.

She made her decision quickly, refusing to consider the danger of attempting to ride an angered horse that had already been subjected to brutal treatment that night. Fighting down an impulse to give in to tears of panic, she went to the gate and picked up the rope, speaking softly to Onyx. Fortunately, he wore a halter; all she had to do was slip the rope through the side of the halter, in a makeshift arrangement of reigns, and hopefully she could guide him. That is, if he would even let her near enough to try.

She slipped quietly through the fence, murmuring under her breath. Every delay was more time wasted, but she knew she had to move slowly, so as not to frighten him into galloping to the other end of the field, or anger him into rearing and striking her before she could move away from him. Moving as slowly as she could, keeping up the murmuring sound, she walked to where the stallion stood, watching her warily. At her approach, he snorted and moved a few feet away. She almost cried out in her impatience, but forced herself to act calmly, moving toward him again.

At last, after two more attempts to come near him, she got close enough to grasp the halter and quickly threaded the rope through, running her hand soothingly down his neck. He laid back his ears and snorted again, jerking his head up with such force that she was lifted off the ground. She held on grimly, knowing that if he managed to get away, she would never catch him again. When he came down on all four feet again, she gently tried to lead him to the fence; he circled around her, laying his ears back and baring his teeth, trying to snatch at her arm. She refused to allow herself to be frightened and climbed the fence rails quickly before he knew what she was going to do.

As she settled herself astride, she felt the huge muscles bunching under her, and grabbed quickly for his mane as he reared under her unaccustomed weight. She clung to him desperately, knowing if she was thrown she had little chance of having him stand for her while she mounted him again. When he came down, she turned him quickly away from the fence, then back again, digging in her heels.

Startled, the stallion leaped forward. Then the fence was almost upon them and she was afraid he was going to crash through. She signaled him again with her heels, urging him forward and at the last moment, she felt him gather himself for the jump. She tightened her hold on his mane as he surged into the air, clearing the fence by at least a foot. They pounded across the field toward the road that led to Hawkshead.

The rain was coming down in earnest now, and strands of hair were plastered across her face, but she did not dare loosen her hold to wipe them away. Never had she ridden an animal that had such speed; he seemed to fly down the road, and she felt exultant as he carried her swiftly toward the house. He seemed to sense her urgency, for he drove himself forward, stretching his neck for greater speed.

In less time than she thought possible, the lights of the house came into view, and then they were sweeping around the side of the house into the stable yard. She pulled on the rope with all her might and the stallion slid to a halt, slipping on the wet ground.

Two grooms came running out from the stables, stopping dead as they recognized the great stallion, but she shouted for them to hold the horse as she threw herself off him and ran to the house.

Running up the back steps, she called to Jergens, scarcely noticing the frightened faces of several of the housemaids as she swept by. Jergens appeared in the hallway, looking startled out of his customary composure as she came panting up to him, gasping that Lord Davencourt was injured. Somehow she managed to tell him enough to let him take charge of the situation with his usual competency. She had a confused impression of Mrs. Murphy's face looming over her, muttering something about not knowing this would happen, then she felt a blackness swiftly rushing over her and pitched forward into the housekeeper's arms.

# CHAPTER FOURTEEN

She returned to consciousness to find Lucy bending over her, wiping her forehead with a cool cloth. Flinging aside the blanket that covered her, she sat up and clutched the girl's arm.

"Did they get to Lord Davencourt in time?" she asked urgently. "Has the doctor been called—is he going to be all right?"

"Yes, miss," Lucy replied quickly. "It's all right. The doctor took the bullet out and thinks the Master will soon be well." Lucy looked at her with admiration in her eyes, and added, "My—we're that proud of you, miss. I know I couldn't have been so brave!"

"It wasn't bravery, Lucy—it was simply urgency," Devon said.

"Well, whatever you say," Lucy answered doubtfully, clearly not convinced. "In any case, you're to go upstairs and right to bed in your old room. You look exhausted."

"No, I can't, Lucy. I must go back to Morehouse. Mrs. Moreland might worry when she finds I'm not there. She must also be told of Lord Davencourt's . . . accident."

"Don't worry about that, miss. Jergens sent one of the lads over, and Mrs. Moreland returned with him. She's waiting in your room to see you."

✻⟐✻

"Devon, I don't know how to thank you," Agatha said when Devon entered her room. Agatha came over to her and embraced her warmly, tears showing in her dark eyes. "But for you, my nephew might have died. We are greatly in your debt."

She held Devon away from her and searched her face. "I don't know what happened there tonight; Gareth is still unconscious—

but I can see from your face that it was a horrible experience. Would you care to tell me about it?" she asked softly.

"First, tell me how Lord Davencourt is," Devon said.

"Dr. Norris managed to remove the bullet without too much injury, but it was lodged fairly close to the lung, so Gareth will have to remain quiet for quite a while," Agatha answered. "Which should upset the household, I should imagine, knowing what a temper he has when confined. But then, he should be thankful that you were able to find help so quickly."

Devon felt such a surge of relief that Lord Davencourt was going to recover that she swayed weakly and was forced to grab Agatha's arm to remain upright. Agatha exclaimed and led her over to the bed where her night things were already laid out and quickly helped her undress and climb into the welcoming bed. A feeling of utter exhaustion stole over her as Agatha pulled the covers over her, but she knew Agatha would want to know the sequence of events that led to Gareth's being shot that night. As briefly as possible, she related the story, beginning with the note that Leticia had written summoning her to a meeting at Onyx's pasture. When she had finished, Agatha sighed and said, "Well, at least the poor woman is past any more trouble now. And to think, none of us was aware that she was losing her mind . . ."

Devon shuddered, remembering how she had last seen Leticia, and Agatha said briskly, "I knew something was going on tonight. Why you didn't see fit to tell me, I'll never know."

"I didn't want to worry you, Agatha. Besides, I knew you would want to come with me, and I didn't want to expose you to any danger."

"Well. I can take care of myself, my girl," Agatha answered, trying to look stern, but succeeding only in appearing gratified. She continued, "I had quite a talk with Mrs. Murphy tonight. It seems that she and Leticia were together in this—to a point. The poor woman was in tears when she confessed that she thought the plan was only to frighten you away; when she found the gun missing, she knew that Leticia was going to try to kill you. Fortunately, she had sense enough to tell Gareth immediately. She said she loved Leticia as a daughter, which I suppose, was why she was as blind as any of us to Leticia's unbalanced state of mind. It was quite a shock for her to hear of Leticia's death—the woman became completely hysterical."

Devon wondered that the frigid Mrs. Murphy could lose control of herself in that way, but suddenly she was so sleepy she could hardly keep her eyes open. She murmured something about pitying the housekeeper, but she could no longer concentrate on what she wanted to say.

Agatha put out the lamp and bent to kiss Devon's forehead. Devon heard her say something, but Agatha's face swam before her heavy eyes and she found herself too tired to respond. She was asleep before Agatha reached the door.

*❋⬦❋*

She woke the next morning to find that the storm from the night before had abated; now the sky was leaden and a steady drizzle blurred the window as she pulled back the draperies and stared out, tying the sash of her robe.

The stable yard below her was a dismal sight, little rivulets of water trickling through the cobblestone path that led to the stables. All the stall doors were closed and no one was in sight, the grooms most likely keeping close to the little stove that burned in the tack room at the far end of the barn. She made a mental note to visit the stables later that day to find out what had been done with Onyx, and as soon as Lord Davencourt recovered she must tell him that the stallion was not responsible for Jeffrey's death, and had in fact saved his own.

She sat on the cushioned window seat, resting her chin on her drawn-up knees, looking blankly down on the deserted yard below her, thinking of Leticia. What had happened to that unfortunate woman to twist her mind into madness, she wondered. Should she, Devon, have been able to recognize the insanity lurking behind those calm eyes, or did madness cloak its insidiousness behind the innocent expression, the tranquil façade—emerging only when the last vestige of reason had gone? She didn't know; she only knew that she felt pity for Leticia Davencourt.

A soft tap on the door interrupted her thoughts; Lucy came in with a tray, which she set on the table. The little maid poured a cup of tea and brought it to her. Devon accepted it with an absent nod, still preoccupied with her thoughts of Leticia.

"Miss?" Lucy asked tentatively, standing before her.

With an effort, Devon forced her attention away from Mrs. Davencourt and turned toward her. "Yes, Lucy."

"Are you feeling all right? You look so pale."

"No, I'm fine, Lucy—just a little tired still, I guess."

"I'm supposed to tell you that the doctor is coming again today. Mrs. Moreland wants you to meet them in the library after breakfast."

Devon's heart missed a beat. "Lord Davencourt—has he taken a turn for the worse?" she asked anxiously.

"I don't know, miss. Mrs. Murphy sat with him all night, and he seems to have a fever . . ." Lucy's small hands twisted the folds of her apron, her eyes filling with tears.

Devon moved to put her arms around the small figure and said, more convincingly than she felt, "You mustn't worry, Lucy. Everything will be all right. Fever is quite common after an injury such as his."

"Do you think so, miss?"

"Certainly," Devon answered confidently, while her heart began an uneasy pounding. She looked about the room to find something to give Lucy to do to keep her occupied. "Now, you can bring me some hot water for a bath, and after that, perhaps you can try to clean that gown I wore last night," she said, indicating the still-sodden garment hanging by the fire.

Lucy hurried over to the dress, clucking in dismay as she pulled it from the chair, and shook it out. She scurried out of the room importantly, her round little face once more with its usual happy expression.

Devon was not so fortunate; she paced up and down the room, trying to overcome the dread she felt. When Lucy brought the hot water, she bathed and dressed quickly in the gown that Mrs. Moreland had had the foresight to bring from her wardrobe and left the room with her breakfast tray untouched and forgotten.

*❋⟐❋*

Agatha was already in the library when Devon arrived, sitting composedly on the sofa. Only her hands, which were clenched tightly in her lap, and the paleness of her strained face, betrayed her worry and anxiety about Gareth.

Devon rushed to her side and sat down next to her. Agatha reached out and grasped her hand tightly and the two women sat in silence, waiting for the doctor's arrival.

The ticking of the clock on the mantel and the steady drip of the rain falling from the eaves were the only sounds in the room. Devon tried not to think of the times she and Lord Davencourt had battled in this room, but the deep leather chair behind the desk, the riding crop thrown carelessly on top, reminded her of him and she could picture him standing there, the hard planes of his face emphasizing the dark eyes that always viewed her with such intensity. She wondered why they had always been at each other's throats; why both of them managed to lose their tempers after five minutes of being in the same room together.

In reflecting on this, she suddenly knew the reason for her own lack of control: her temper was merely a façade to cover her true emotions. Her feelings for him, ever on the surface, must be covered up, so that she would not expose herself to his mockery when he learned that she loved him. Yes, she thought—in my pride, I must hide the one thing that means the most to me, so that I will not be made to feel like a fool. Well, the opportunity, if ever there was one, was lost now. She had only herself to blame.

She was so engrossed in her thoughts that she did not hear the doctor come in; was aware of his presence only when Agatha stood up and addressed him in a tightly controlled voice.

"My dear Agatha," he said, bowing slightly, "what a terrible time for you . . ."

"Yes, yes," Agatha interrupted, drawing herself up regally. "You can dispense with any condolences for the time being, and get to the heart of the matter. Is my nephew going to be all right?"

Evidently Dr. Norris was accustomed to Agatha's somewhat withering manner, for he said calmly, "I have just finished my examination. The situation is serious"—he held up his hand as a cry escaped Agatha's lips—"but I think he will recover nicely in time. I took it upon myself to engage a nurse from London; she should arrive today, or at the latest, tomorrow morning."

Dr. Norris looked at Devon, who had stood in white-faced silence during the conversation, and said, "He owes his life to you, my dear. He might have bled to death but for your prompt action, Miss Brandwyne. It seems that you are the heroine of the hour. Now—I presume you both wish to see him?"

He looked at Agatha, who nodded, then he said, "Only for a moment. He is still not out of danger and very weak." His eyes twinkled as he added, "But don't tell him I said that or he will insist on getting up just to prove me wrong!"

Devon followed Agatha up the stairs and when the woman indicated she should go in first, Devon shook her head. "No, I am sure he will want to see you, Agatha—and I know you are concerned about him. I will wait."

Agatha was in the room only a few minutes and when she came out, Mrs. Murphy, who had been sitting with Lord Davencourt, followed. Devon was surprised at the change in the housekeeper; she no longer appeared so coldly arrogant—in fact, she thought, Mrs. Murphy seemed to have shriveled somehow, and her eyes when she raised them to Devon's face had a blank despairing look. Mrs. Murphy started to say something to Devon, but changed her mind and went off down the hall with bowed head. Poor woman, Devon said to herself, she must have loved Leticia Davencourt dearly to be so sunk in grief. But she forgot the housekeeper entirely as she went into Lord Davencourt's room.

She stood by the bed, looking down at Gareth. A lock of black hair had fallen on to his forehead, emphasizing the extreme pallor of his face; the high cheekbones seemed to strain against his skin. Dark shadows appeared almost purple under his eyes and his breathing was so shallow that for a moment Devon feared that he might be dead.

He seemed to sense her presence, for in a moment, he stirred and opened his eyes, looking up at her. His hand moved on top of the thick quilts that covered him, and she grasped it with her own, trying to keep back tears as he pressed her fingers weakly.

"Devon," he said in a voice that was like a sigh.

"I'm here, Gareth," she said softly. "Everything is going to be all right."

"I'm glad you weren't hurt," he whispered. "I should have known it was Leticia . . . there were signs . . ." He frowned and a spasm of pain crossed his features, causing white ridges to spring out about his mouth. When the spasm passed, he continued halt-

ingly, "You are free to go now—your mystery has been solved. But
. . . I wanted to thank you . . . Dr. Norris said you saved my life
—and if there is anything I can do . . . to repay you, you have
only to ask . . ."

His eyes closed in exhaustion, and Devon looked at him sadly,
wondering if she would ever be able to forget him and love
another man as much as she loved him. She longed to put her
arms around him and hold him fiercely to her, but his words
tolled like a death knell in her mind: "you are free to go now . . ."
The last hope died in her, and she knew she must waste no time
in leaving Hawkshead. She wondered that she felt so little pain in
the thought; she felt almost empty inside, as though all emotion
had dried up. Later though, when she had time to reflect—time
to get over the shock of Leticia's death and the horror of her experiences—then, she knew, she would be tormented by the
thought of leaving Gareth. Yes, it was best that she leave immediately before she should weaken. It was obvious that Gareth
wanted her to leave, and she would do that last thing for him.

She knew that he had only to say one word to keep her here;
one word that would evaporate the pride that had kept her silent,
unable to admit aloud her love for him. But no; he had said she
was free to go now, so that was what she would do. Having come
to this decision, she looked at Gareth for the last time, and felt
the first inkling of the hurt she would endure. Refusing to allow
herself the luxury of giving in to her pain, she squared her shoulders and passed through the door, being careful not to look back.

✳❧✳

There was no sign of Agatha when she came out into the hall,
and she was thankful that she did not have to face the woman
yet. Her feelings were held in check under such brittle control
that she knew she had only to hear one comforting word from
Agatha and her calmness would shatter completely.

She went to her room and gathered what few articles remained
there. She went down the stairs, intending to find Jergens and ask
him to have one of the grooms drive her back to Morehouse.
Once her trunk was packed, she was certain she could face Agatha
calmly and tell her she was leaving.

Jergens and Mrs. Murphy stood in the hall, conversing in low tones. When Mrs. Murphy saw Devon coming toward them, she excused herself and came over to her. "Miss Brandwyne, I can't tell you how sorry I am that I helped to put you in such danger," she began, raising troubled eyes that held no trace of their former glacial expression.

Devon felt that the housekeeper had suffered enough, knowing that by abetting Leticia in her scheme she had brought such disaster upon the household. She had no wish to contribute to the woman's obvious distress by refusing to accept her apology. She said, "I'm sure you had no knowledge of the extent of Lady Davencourt's plans, Mrs. Murphy. I think the important thing right now is to assure Lord Davencourt's recovery, not dwell on past mistakes. After all, we were all involved to some degree."

The housekeeper looked at her in surprise, unwilling to believe that Devon could forgive her so easily. Devon smiled at her and started forward to ask Jergens about the transportation she desired when she heard carriage wheels on the drive.

Through the window, she could see Lady Elinor step down from the carriage and hurry up the front steps. She swept into the house as if she already owned it, and seeing Devon in the hall, rushed over to her and demanded, "And what are *you* doing here, pray? I thought you had taken yourself away by this time."

Devon answered stiffly, "I was just about to do so, Lady Elinor."

"Excellent. I don't want you and all the trouble you have caused interfering with Gareth's recovery. I want you to leave Hawkshead without delay—do you understand?"

"Perfectly," Devon said.

The two women stared at each other and suddenly Devon no longer felt anything but pity for Elinor Chadmoore. If Gareth wanted a woman who had such an exaggerated idea of her own importance, then he was welcome to her. Elinor Chadmoore might be beautiful, be possessed of a charm and poise that were enviable, but inside she was an empty shell, concerned with only her own wants and desires. She would always take from others, giving nothing in return except what was absolutely necessary for the continuous adulation she so desired. And if that was what

Gareth wanted in a woman, then he was not the kind of man she, Devon, had thought.

Lady Elinor was looking at her strangely, as if she had some inkling of the thoughts that were going through her mind. Her expression became suddenly crude, and now Devon had no wish to engage in another verbal battle. She said, "I did want to tell you that I wish you and Lord Davencourt every happiness in your marriage."

Elinor looked askance at Devon for a moment before saying, "Why, yes. To be sure. Thank you, Miss Brandwyne." Caught off guard by Devon's remark, she hesitated again, as though she wanted to say something else, but she changed her mind and turned away from Devon, gesturing to Mrs. Murphy to follow her before she bustled importantly up the stairs.

Devon watched her go, feeling nothing but emptiness, and then when Jergens tapped her on the arm, saying that the carriage was ready to take her back to Morehouse, she thanked him bleakly and walked out of Hawkshead.

# CHAPTER FIFTEEN

Cecily was surprised the night Devon appeared on her doorstep without warning, but had received her with open arms and a great deal of curiosity, which fortunately for Devon, she kept to herself. She was a new Cecily, a more mature woman, who took one look at Devon's strained face and shadowed eyes and insisted on putting her to bed in her old room without asking for any explanations.

The next day she came into Devon's room to help her unpack and asked only one question: Did you love him so very much? Devon was surprised at the astuteness of the question; no more the gay, lighthearted silly girl was Cecily—but a young matron, her figure becoming rounder as she and Edgar awaited the birth of their first child—a Cecily who was more understanding, more compassionate.

Devon shied away from the answer to Cecily's question and knew by her sister's sympathy-filled eyes that she did not have to answer. After that day, Cecily asked no more, and for Devon the time had not come when she felt able to talk about her experiences at Hawkshead.

For Devon's sake, her sister gave small dinner parties, always making certain there was at least one eligible male present. But Devon, though polite, was restrained in company, and many of Cecily's friends commented privately to Cecily on her sister's quietness. Cecily just shook her head and refused to enlighten them, blithely insisting that nothing was wrong to protect Devon from their probing curiosity.

Devon took long walks to occupy herself, but the bustle of the

London outskirts was disquieting to her after the serene countryside surrounding Hawkshead, and soon she found herself dread-
ing to leave the house. In vain, she appealed to Cecily to allow
her to take over some of the chores of the household, but Cecily
replied that everything ran so smoothly with the housekeeper that
Edgar had engaged, that there was really nothing to do in that
quarter.

Devon grew more pale and quiet daily, and finally in desperation at her sister's listlessness, Cecily appealed to Edgar, who in
turn offered Devon one of his horses to ride whenever she chose.
Devon accepted the offer gratefully, and rode every day, but even
this could not remove the ache in her heart, nor stop her eyes
from searching for a man who she knew she would never see
again.

She acquired a translucent quality that seemed to appeal, for in
spite of her aloofness, several young men came to call upon her, or
made offers to take her to the theater. She accepted several times
to please Cecily, who had begun to look at her anxiously, but she
was always relieved when the evening was over and she did not
have to concentrate on a young man's conversation that she had
no interest in.

She knew she should begin to search for another post, but a
state of lethargy concerning her life had settled on her and she
found she could do nothing except move through one empty day
after another.

One day, when she had been "home" almost three weeks, she
received a letter from Agatha Moreland. Feeling the first bit of excitement she had experienced since leaving Hawkshead, she seized
it eagerly and read:

My dear Devon,

I hope this letter finds you well and recovered from your terrible experience. As I told you when you informed me that you
were returning to your sister's home, I do not understand why
you felt it necessary to leave. But then, you are old enough to
manage your own affairs and I must respect your judgment—
reluctantly. Let me say, however, that I do miss you . . .

Naturally, there was quite a bit of fuss when the police came to take statements concerning Leticia's death and Gareth's near-fatal wound, but my nephew's wishes—as usual —prevailed, as he would not allow you to be called for the inquest. The verdict was accidental death, and Gareth has handled the resulting scandal and gossip that followed it by ignoring the whole thing in public, and raging against it in private. At any rate, the whole affair is dying down at last.

As for Gareth, he is recovering nicely—the wound, that is —his temper has not improved with his enforced confinement and daily I expect to hear reports of the servants moving out en masse. Occasionally I have Robbie drive me to Hawkshead and confess that I have actually condescended to plead patience with Jergens and Cook in order to convince them to weather this storm.

Well, enough of that. I find Gareth exceedingly tiresome as a convalescent and can only hope for all our sakes he manages to get well immediately.

I do wish you would consider a visit, Devon. You know you are always welcome at Morehouse.

Agatha Moreland

Devon read and reread the letter several times before folding it and putting it away in her desk. How thoughtful of Agatha to write her about Gareth's recovery—but it was just like her to omit any mention of Lady Elinor, she thought wryly. Perhaps the omission was to spare her; she supposed the wedding plans were proceeding apace and Agatha did not want to stir up old feelings. Sometime in the future, when she was certain she could view Hawkshead and its inhabitants dispassionately, she would consider Agatha's offer of a visit. But not just yet.

Another month passed. Flowers were blooming in profusion in Cecily's little garden at the back of the house, and the trees were taking on a greenish cast as their leaves unfolded. The air smelled fresh and clean in the early mornings when Devon customarily went for her daily ride. This was the best part of the day for her;

cantering along as the sun rose through the trees, she could almost forget Gareth.

It was time to begin searching for a position, she thought one morning when she had returned to the house after her ride. The trite expression—time will heal—popped into her head, and though eight weeks ago she would have denied it, today she was almost convinced it was true. After breakfast she would send a message to the solicitor, Mr. Pream, to ask if he could help her once again.

She was in her room, changing from her riding habit, when Cecily burst in without knocking. Devon looked at her in surprise; her sister's round face was flushed with excitement and her blond curls tumbled about her shoulders as though she hadn't taken time to brush them that morning.

Devon gently led her to a chair, fearing that all this agitation might be bad for the coming baby, and said, "Cecily, you must calm yourself. Is something the matter? Should I call a doctor?"

Cecily put her hand to her heart and gasped, "No, I'm fine—I just ran up the stairs, I was so excited! Devon, you have a visitor!"

Startled, Devon asked, "Well, for heaven's sake, who is it?"

For a moment, the young Cecily stared at her, eyes twinkling mischievously, all the new maturity gone. She said, "You'll have to go down and see; I'm not going to tell you."

Devon could have shaken her in her impatience to learn the identity of the visitor, but Cecily looked so young and happy, she smiled instead. She thought: Who could have caused all this excitement? Certainly not any of the young men Cecily had been busily introducing her to these past two months. Then she knew: Agatha Moreland! She remembered how impressed she had been at her first sight of the regal Mrs. Moreland, and she couldn't blame Cecily for the same reaction.

She finished dressing quickly, eager to run downstairs and greet Agatha. Cecily sat in the chair, eyes sparkling, and jumped up just as Devon was going out the door, coming over to give Devon's hair a final pat into place. Suddenly Cecily leaned forward and kissed her on the cheek, saying, "Remember, Devon, don't be so stiff-necked and proud," before she pushed her out the door.

For a moment Devon was puzzled at this remark, but she forgot Cecily's words as she ran down the stairs, eager for a reunion with Agatha.

She swept into the sitting room and almost stumbled on the threshold as she saw who the visitor was.

Gareth Davencourt turned from the window where he had been standing, staring moodily out at the street below. They stared at each other in silence, and Devon knew it had been the utmost folly for her to try to convince herself that she had forgotten him. All she had to do was see him standing there and all the weeks of carefully not thinking about him were lost. Her heart pounded uncomfortably, and her throat was dry; for a horrible moment she thought she was going to faint.

Wordlessly, she gestured to a chair and forced herself to sit down opposite him, using all her control to keep her expression politely interested in the occasion of his visit. His dark eyes were close to hers as he leaned forward, but still he said nothing. The silence was unbearable to her; she knew she must speak, but she was afraid the only sound she would be able to make would be a croak.

At last she managed to say, "I see you have recovered, Lord Davencourt," and thought what a mundane remark it was when all the time she wanted to cry out: Why did you come again, when I had just convinced myself that I could go on without you!

"No, I have not recovered," he answered, frowning, and she looked at him in surprise. He grimaced slightly and continued, "I told you once that I would not grovel before any woman, and I will not. But for once, you will listen to what I have to say—God knows I have had enough time to think of it—and this time you will hear me out . . ."

He stopped talking and sprang up, pacing back and forth, as if what he had to say was distasteful and he did not know how to go about it. She watched him in silence, wondering what it was that seemed so difficult for him to tell her.

At last he turned to her and said abruptly, "I will try to understand if you refuse me, but I must have your answer now. These past two months have been unendurable—and I refuse to go on this way . . . Damn it—what I'm trying to say is that I want you to marry me." He stopped pacing and looked down at her, his whole manner tense as he waited for her response.

A wild feeling of elation rose in her and she wanted to laugh triumphantly and throw herself into his arms, but though she knew what this had cost him in pride, she wanted him to say the words she had thought never to hear from him. She said demurely, looking at him from beneath lowered lashes, "I take it this is a royal command?"

He stiffened and his face turned crimson with the effort to control his temper. At last he said in a choked voice, "Devon, do not play games with me. I had hoped you loved me, but I can see now I was in error. Forgive me for the intrusion."

In spite of herself, she could feel her temper flaring; she stood up, and with eyes flashing, said, "Is it so difficult to say the words? You have asked—no, told—me to marry you, but though you spoke of love on my part, I have not heard you mention the word in your own regard. I . . ."

In one step his arms were around her and his head bent until he stared straight into her eyes. "You little fool—don't you know I have loved you from the moment I first saw you? If you need to hear me say it, I will. I love you—I will always love you, my little spitfire. Now, will you marry me?"

She looked into the black eyes so close to her own and whispered, "Yes. Oh, Gareth—yes!"

"Excellent," came a dry voice from the doorway. Gareth exclaimed impatiently, but did not release his hold on Devon as Agatha Moreland swept into the room.

"Agatha! I thought I told you to wait in the carriage," Gareth grated as Agatha came over to kiss Devon's cheek.

"So you did, nephew," Agatha said serenely, taking Devon's arm and leading her over to the sofa. "But I wouldn't have missed this for the world—I've been waiting for you two to make up your minds far too long as it is!"

She looked at Devon, and then both of them laughed at Gareth's furious expression. "Oh, Devon," Agatha said gaily. "You should have seen him—in a temper all the time because he could not beat down his pride long enough to come and ask you to marry him. I told him often enough that he was being pig-headed and stubborn, but. . . ."

"That's enough, Agatha," Gareth said in mock anger, "or you will turn her head. I think I shall have quite enough trouble trying to manage that terrible temper of hers without her knowing all my secrets!"

"Ah, yes. But what fun!" Agatha exclaimed. "Well, Devon, if you will introduce me to that sister of yours, perhaps she and I can admire the garden—or something—while you two make your plans."

As soon as the introductions had been made and Gareth and Devon were alone again, Gareth swept her into his arms. For an instant, Devon held back and Gareth frowned. "What is the matter now? Have you changed your mind?" he teased.

"No. But I have to ask you about Elinor Chadmoore before I can be absolutely certain," she said seriously.

"What about her?"

She felt that she might be risking all her new-found happiness, but she knew she could not live with the shadow of Elinor over her. "Were you in love with her?"

He hesitated, then said, "She was my mistress for a time—but not after I had met you."

"And the baby?"

"How did you know about that? Never mind . . . women have a way of ferreting out these things, I suppose . . . No, the child was not mine, though she tried to convince me it was. Anyway, Elinor finally realized I would have no part of her—and I suppose she is consoling herself in the arms of a marquis somewhere on the Continent. But why ask about her? You might give me some explanation about Courtney—you two were as thick as thieves."

His brows drew together in a frown and she laughed, "Don't tell me you were jealous!"

"No. I simply considered calling him out when he had the effrontery to ask you to marry him!"

"How did you find out about that? Never mind, men have a way . . . at any rate, you needn't have worried—I was in love with someone else at the time," she said, running her finger along his hard jaw.

They talked for some time, and Devon felt as though she could not have enough of the sight of him. She learned that Gareth had been suspicious of Leticia for some time, but could never obtain any proof that she was responsible for the things that had happened to Devon. When Mrs. Murphy had come to him and warned him about the meeting Leticia had contrived with Devon that horrible night, he knew immediately that she was in danger; he had hurried to the scene barely in time to stop Leticia's mad scheme.

"And that is another thing," he said, looking sternly at her, "if I hadn't known that I wanted you for my wife, seeing you get on Onyx and take that fence would have convinced me that I had to have you. I knew I would have to take you in hand"—he paused and added smilingly—"if only to save you from your own stubbornness. Now, may I kiss my future wife?"

�֎ᘓ�֎

They were married in a small ceremony one week later in the drawing room in Cecily and Edgar's home. For a wedding present, Gareth had given her a necklace of perfectly matched emeralds, which had been handed down for two centuries to the bride of the Master of Hawkshead. But the proudest moment of Devon's life was when Gareth slipped the heavy heirloom wedding ring with the Hawkshead crest encrusted with diamonds and emeralds on her finger. Devon had looked at him with tears of happiness glistening in her eyes, and he had responded with a smile so loving that she felt she would dissolve in the joy she felt. She knew that two such strong-willed and stubborn people as she and Gareth would have many stormy times in their marriage; but with sudden maturity, she knew she would overcome and learn to control her hasty temper and perhaps smooth the way for her proud and sometimes overbearing husband. She had never been so happy.

They had decided to delay the honeymoon and return to Hawkshead after the wedding. Gareth wanted to engage a competent steward to supervise the many facets of the estate in his absence—especially the new breeding farm he had started with the purchase of Onyx. Devon was content to wait; she must make the transition to Mistress of Hawkshead, and in so doing, earn the confidence and support of the servants.

As the carriage turned into the long drive and the house came into view, Devon reflected that Hawkshead no longer seemed sinister to her. A pall had been lifted with the death of Leticia; Jeffrey's ghost had been laid to rest, and Devon knew the house would never again seem forbidding. She looked at Gareth, who took her hand and smiled as though he could read her thoughts.

All the servants were waiting in the courtyard as Gareth assisted Devon from the carriage. Lucy came forward with a huge bouquet of roses, her face shining with happiness as she curtsied deeply and handed them to her.

Devon accepted the flowers with a smile that betrayed her own inner joy. She glanced up at Gareth, who bent and murmured in her ear, "I knew you would prefer an unconventional wedding present—look!"

She followed the direction of his glance and saw the head groom walking toward her, leading the bay mare she had thought had been destroyed after her accident that first day at Hawkshead. Flowers were entwined in the mane of the prancing mare, and a coal-black foal scampered by her side.

Gareth said softly, an unmistakable note of pride in his voice, "The mare—and I'm certain you remember her—is called Firelight, and the foal is the first sired by Onyx. They are yours—the beginning of the Hawkshead Thoroughbreds, which together we will make a name to be reckoned with."

"Oh, Gareth," Devon breathed as she reached out and touched the velvety soft muzzle of the mare, the baby-fine hair on the foal's neck. A sudden suspicion made her turn accusingly to Gareth and ask, "How could you know we would be married? That the gift of the mare would please me above all? You took her away and hid her on purpose, didn't you? You planned this all along!"

Gareth laughed and put his arm tenderly about her waist, drawing her closer to him. He said, without a trace of his usual mockery, "Of course, my darling. I am rarely wrong!"